Fallin' for a hustler like me

Natisha Raynor

Blake Karrington

Chapter One

"What the fuck are you doing?" Khelani asked through clenched teeth as she trained her Glock on Malachi. She stared at the sight before her with a shattered heart, but she would be damned if she let a single tear fall from her eyes.

Malachi looked over his shoulder, and when he saw her standing there with a gun trained on him, his left eyebrow hiked up. Temporarily abandoning the treasure before him, Malachi stood up and turned around to face Khelani. There really was no way for him to explain what he was doing with her safe opened. Thirty pounds of weed and a few stacks of cash stared him in the face. From the moment the door swung open, he had to decide between leaving the weed and money there or crossing Khelani and robbing her. He was in a jam. A jam that could cost him his life. He owed someone a lot of money and rather than just being a man and coming to Khelani to maybe get fronted some work, he was going to take the grimy route and rob her. Right after fucking her, he planned to get what he needed while she was in the shower, dip, and explain

1

himself later, but his plans had been ruined. He didn't miss the pained expression that was etched on Khelani's face or the hurt that lie in her grey eyes. He was trying to survive. It wasn't anything personal. Maybe he'd be able to convince her of that, but he could tell from the way she was glaring at him that wouldn't be an easy task.

"Khelani I know how this looks but just let me explain." Funny thing was, after that, he was quiet. He wasn't saying anything. Because he didn't have anything to say. How was he going to explain what he was doing in her safe and make it sound believable? Khelani was far from dumb.

His lack of words did it for her. He was going to die anyway, but as soon as he hesitated with his explanation, Khelani pumped his body full of bullets. The bullets made his body jerk slightly before he fell backwards into the wall. Khelani watched as his body slid down the wall as traces of his blood stained the paint. His eyes were locked on hers the entire time. As soon as his bottom tapped the floor, blood spilled from his mouth, and his head fell to the left. He was dead.

Khelani backed out of the room and headed for the bathroom where her phone was located. With trembling hands, she picked it up from the sink and called Kasim. He would know what to do. She wasn't about to say too much over the phone, but as soon as he heard her voice crack, he knew she was indeed in trouble. Khelani wasn't the one to show emotion, and Kasim dropped everything he was doing to rush to her. It was a good thing he only lived one block over. He was there in no time and when she took him to Malachi's body, he knew what he had to do.

"What happened? Are you okay?" he looked her over and saw that she was only dressed in a black silk robe.

"He tried to fuckin' rob me. That's what happened," Khelani replied with a hint of anger in her tone.

"You're too powerful, Khelani. You'll never find a man unless you submit. No man can take you outshining him," she mocked the words that Kasim spoke to her months before.

"Now you see why I don't let men get close to me?" she snapped.

Khelani walked away and left Kasim to clean up the mess she'd made. Her father told her not to come to the states and fall in love. Love and money didn't mix, and she was to always no matter what choose the money over love. Khelani placed her hands on the back of her neck and blew out air as she looked up at the ceiling. For the first time in a long time she had started to like someone, and it had ended with her painting the wall with his blood. It only confirmed what she already knew. She couldn't trust any fuckin' body, and love wasn't for her.

Kyrie Richmond pulled up at the location his partner Ghalen had provided him with. He pulled around to the very back of the warehouse. It was pitch black out, but Kyrie spotted Ghalen's Audi right away. He also noticed Montana's motorcycle. Montana was the head of Kyrie's security team. Kyrie shut the engine off and looked over at Taina.

"I'll be right back," he told his date of the evening. She nodded, and Kyrie emerged from the car.

She had no clue where they were, but she wasn't afraid. She wasn't afraid because she had never seen the dark side of Kyrie. She only knew him as the head of a successful record label. Taina didn't know about Kyrie's street dealings. She had no clue what he was doing at a warehouse that looked desolate, but she didn't care. Taina just wanted him to hurry back to her, so they could go back to her place. It was only their first date, but she wanted to fuck. No questions asked. To be on the arm of a man like Kyrie was a privilege in itself. She didn't take any pictures with him and post them herself, because she didn't want to seem like a groupie. But Taina prayed that someone would snap a picture of them and post her on a blog. Not only did she hope to get in good with Kyrie but being on the arm of a man of his caliber would make other rich niggas want her. The shit was weird, but that's how it worked. There was a reason IG models got passed around the industry. If a man saw his peer fucking with a bad bitch that was about her bread, it would stroke that man's ego if the same female gave him the time of day. Being spotted out with Kyrie would make her stock go up for sure.

Oblivious to the mental plotting that his date was doing, Kyrie walked swiftly to the back door and as if Montana could sense his presence, he swung the door open for Kyrie.

"What up boss?" Montana gave Kyrie dap before leading him further into the room.

Kyrie smiled when he saw a man tied a chair. The chair sat in the middle of the empty space, and Ghalen stood in front of the chair with a shiny object in his hand. Kyrie walked over to Ghalen and gave him dap before taking the $65,000 chain from him.

Once the necklace was in his hand, he glared over at the man in the chair. His eyes were almost swollen shut. His nose was crooked, letting Kyrie know that it was broken, and there was a huge lump on his forehead. He'd been beaten senseless for sure.

"What made you think it was a good idea to rob one of my artists for his chain? Then you took it a step further and tried to make him pay you to get it back. Big bad ass gangsta nigga." Kyrie turned to look at Ghalen. "This can't be the same nigga that was on his snapchat boasting and bragging about taking Kilo's chain. He's real quiet right now."

Ghalen smirked. "That's because he's missing a few teeth."

Kyrie turned his attention back to the man in the chair. "Damn they fucked you up. You know, on the way over here, I had all kinds of devious thoughts. I almost stopped by my crib to get my ax because the idea of cutting your thieving ass hand off excited me. I mean damn near made my dick hard. But I'm a businessman. I'm not savage ass Kyrie anymore, and I won't risk a murder charge for me or anyone in my camp. So, you better thank God that I'm choosing to let you live. But don't be shy now. Don't stay off snap 'cus you all fucked up. Show your face and let your viewers know how robbing Kilo turned out for you. Sucka ass nigga," Kyrie growled before walking off. "Let this bitch go," he instructed Montana.

Montana eyed the man that was barely clinging to life. He understood very well why Kyrie didn't want to risk having the man killed. It was no secret that he robbed Kyrie's artist, and if he turned up dead, that would bring heat to Kyrie and his team. It was something that they didn't need. But Montana had been in the streets for years, and he just didn't think letting this kid live was smart. Kyrie was the boss though, and he had to do what he was told. He just hoped that not following his gut wouldn't come back to bite him or Kyrie in the ass.

Chapter Two

Two months later........

"I really wish you would call dad," Khelani stated as she walked into the living room and saw her sister Anya stretched out on the couch eating yogurt.

Anya peered at her sister as she placed diamond studs into her ear. "You look nice." She took in the black high waist slacks that hugged Khelani's hips, and her red silk blouse. Khelani was barefoot, and the red polish on her toes matched the shirt she wore perfectly. Her thick dark curly hair was pulled up into a high bun.

"Thank you but you not acknowledging what I said doesn't mean that I won't say it again. He always calls my phone when you don't answer for him. I'm a little sick of being the messenger for two people who are capable of talking for themselves."

Anya groaned and rolled her eyes dramatically. "Call him for whatttt? All he's going to do is threaten to make me come back to Trinidad as if I'm not a grown woman. He's the fuckin' fun police," she grumbled, and Khelani shook her head.

"Anya we were sent to the states for a reason. We knew from day one that we were supposed to be here working. But no matter where we go, I'm always the one working, and you just bullshit."

"Because I'm not a slave. I never even said I wanted to be a drug dealer. He can't just make us sell his shit," Anya stated with a face full of disdain.

At twenty-three, Anya was still young, but Khelani felt that it was time for her to grow up. They'd been in the states for two years. After they set up shop in North Carolina and got a steady line of income coming in for their father who was the plug back in Trinidad, they hit the road to take over Atlanta next. Their father Kemp was a very powerful man, and he didn't send them to the states alone. That would be too much like feeding them to the wolves. They had a driver, Kasim, that also doubled as their muscle. Once they got settled, it became very clear to Khelani that she was a one woman show. All Anya cared about was having fun, partying, and fucking.

"Daddy sent us to North Carolina with $300,000 and four hundred pounds of weed. Us getting set up in North Carolina was his money, but this condo," Khelani swept her hand around "this $2,500 a month condo came from all the drugs *I* sold. The allowance he sent you last month was just that, an allowance, because you damn sure don't earn the shit."

"And you never mess up right? The last time I checked you were the one who almost fucked shit up for us the last time, not me."

"I may have fucked shit up, but I still got the job done. All you did was sleep all day and party all night. It's not going that way this time. So, get off your ass and start helping me, and start answering dad's phone calls, today. You have until the end of the month or I'm making a phone call of my own," Khelani pointed at her sister.

Khelani stood 5'7 with dark brown skin and the most beautiful grey eyes. She was thicker than a bowl of oatmeal and a no nonsense kind of woman. As she eyed her sister with skin the color of heavily creamed coffee and grey eyes that mirrored hers, all she could do was shake her head. Anya stood a little taller at 5'8 and had more than a handful of hips. She was a beauty indeed. But she was also a big brat. Not only was their father's drug empire Khelani's business, but she had to spend her free time baby-sitting Anya, and she was over it.

"Why should I have to earn it when my father is a multimillionaire? Make it make sense?" Anya snapped like the spoiled brat that she was. "You just defend him all the time because you're his favorite."

"Nah, I'm just tired of doing all the work while you reap the benefits. I made $54,000 yesterday off pounds, and I'm still up bright and early to go to my first day of a job that I don't fuckin' need but making the right connections in this city will be worth my while. And if I'm dad's favorite then you're damn sure mom's."

"It's goes beyond having a favorite. He has always treated you like the perfect child. It's no secret that you're his heart and he hates me."

"He doesn't hate you, Anya. You're just irresponsible and you make it hard for everyone around you. How do you think I feel knowing that you're our mother's favorite? All because you have light skin like hers. She acts like I'm so ugly just because of my dark skin. Adelyn is a colorist and that's what I don't fuck with."

"You are reaching."

"Am I?"

Khelani's phone rang before either of them could say another word. She looked down and saw that it was her father calling again. He was the last person to call her the night before and the first person calling her this morning. Khelani let out an air of irritation before answering the call and placing it on speakerphone.

"Hey daddy. I only have ten minutes before I have to leave out for work. You're on speaker phone. Anya is right here."

Anya's eyes widened at her sister's betrayal. Kemp cleared his throat and when he spoke, his voice boomed through the speaker on the phone. "I'm pretty sure that my money is what pays your cell phone bill, and since you can't answer my calls, I won't pay the bill. I sent you with your sister to be an asset not a liability, and there's no need to get mad at your sister. She works for *me*. Kasim works for *me*, and when I ask them a question about your behavior, I expect an answer. They are not to cover for you. You're cut off. Until you can prove to me why I should be sending you $3,000 a month, you won't get another penny from me."

The call ended, and Anya was so angry that she was seeing red. In her ungrateful world, $3,000 wasn't shit. She didn't have to pay rent, utilities, car payment, or even her own cell phone bill, so her entire monthly allowance went towards, clothes, shoes, hair, and nails. She didn't even consider the fact that if she'd help Khelani the way she was supposed to, she'd be making more money, and that would be enough to afford her the luxurious lifestyle that she wanted to live, but Anya wanted everything handed to her.

Khelani knew that her sister would be angry for a minute, so she went to her bedroom, stuck her feet into her red Louboutin heels and grabbed her purse. She left the apartment and headed to the parking garage where her burnt orange 2021 BMW x5 was parked. For her first day as an administrative assistant at a record label, she didn't want Kasim to drive her. Kemp was a rich and powerful man and since he didn't have the son he wanted, he groomed Khelani to be as savage as any nigga. He saw to it that she was educated, well spoken, could shoot a gun, cook a brick, and eyeball a gram of weed before she could drive. His businesses in Trinidad were so lucrative that when he decided to take over the states, he didn't send one of his henchmen, he sent his daughters.

Khelani was to play it safe. She couldn't just show up in town and start moving work. She would blend in with the right crowds, entertain the right people, and develop business relationships. She'd then become their supplier and open up the pipeline for them to deal with Kemp's people directly. Since marijuana had become legal in a few states, Kemp had way more competition now than he did years ago. He had to match the high quality of the weed that was now so easily accessible in the states, and he had to have plenty of it at competitive prices. Khelani felt that getting in good with rappers and high profile businessmen in Atlanta would be her best move. Her resume was impressive. She had never worked a "real job," but she used Kemp's legal businesses as references. With her stellar resume and her good looks, she was hired on the spot. Khelani knew that it was important to show up and show out. She had to prove that she was a boss bitch and not just some groupie looking to fuck her way to the top.

Khelani pulled up to a tall building that was located Uptown, about twenty minutes later and parked her car. The streets were crowded, and everyone seemed to have somewhere to be. Grabbing her purse off the passenger seat, Khelani opened her door and stepped outside of the car. She tossed her purse over her shoulder and then closed her door and hit the lock button on her key fob before following a few other people inside of the large building. As soon as she walked in, she saw the place was even busier than the streets had been. Khelani looked all around trying to remember what floor she needed to be on. From her understanding, the record label didn't own the entire building, but they occupied four floors. The building had ten floors total.

"Hey, Khelani right?" She immediately remembered that the man approaching her was the person who interviewed her, and she offered him a big smile.

Ghalen was 5'10 and he had a stocky build. His skin reminded her of dark chocolate and his long dreads were braided up and hanging down his back. He wore an expensive black suit and an even more expensive pair of black shoes. Ghalen looked like the definition of distinguished. His cologne infiltrated her nose, and she even peeped that his nails were neat, short, and manicured.

"Yes, that's correct."

"Nice to see you again. Kyrie is really excited to have you join the team. Ninety-percent of the staff here is black. People might hear the words record label and automatically think about diamond chains and a bunch of niggas walking around in sagging jeans, but that's not the case here. This label makes Kyrie a lot of money, and he takes it very very seriously. Professionalism is a must. Knowing your job is a must. He doesn't mind helping his own but coming to work and doing things half-assed is like not coming at all. I'm the accountant, but I'm on the third floor where you will be. I will introduce you to the office manager Kim. She will train you and get you all set up."

"Okay and thank you so much. Sounds good to me." Khelani followed Ghalen onto the elevator.

The elevator stopped on the second floor, and a pretty black woman wearing a form fitting black dress and a black headwrap got on. She gave a small head nod to Khelani and Ghalen. Atlanta was nothing short of amazing to Khelani.

Every city had boss bitches, but Atlanta took it to another level. It truly was the black mecca. Khelani was a boss bitch in her own right, and no other woman intimidated her. She liked seeing women on their shit, but she also knew women could be catty, envious beings that liked to keep some shit going. She was giving this job six weeks. Since she'd only been in Atlanta for a month, she didn't have a lot of clientele, so she wasn't really missing out on money by being at the job, but she didn't need the job. She was there for a reason, and she couldn't bullshit with that reason. She'd do a good job while she was employed there but when she made the connections she came for, she was gone.

The elevator stopped on the third floor, and all three occupants stepped off. Ghalen introduced Khelani to Kim, and then he went on about his business. Kim was a brown-skinned woman that stood 5'7 without heels, and her hair was in long locs that hung down her back, and the tips were dyed blonde. Khelani hadn't worn heels in a minute, and by the time Kim was done giving her a tour of the third floor, her feet were throbbing. The job didn't sound too complicated and she was sure that she'd get the hang of it in no time. Khelani was smart as hell and a fast learner. After the tour was a walk-through all of the software on the computer, how to use it, and what was expected of her each day. Every time someone walked by, Kim would stop them and make introductions. Two hours later, Kim was done, and Khelani was mentally exhausted.

"I pushed back a meeting to be able to get this done with you. I have to go. Do you think you'll be okay out here alone? I have to meet with some record execs, and that will probably take me about two hours."

"Oh, I'll be fine," Khelani assured her as she glanced at her computer screen and saw that she had nine new emails for the email address that had been set up for her.

"Good. Email me if you need me, and you can go ahead and take a fifteen minute break. At one, you can take your hour lunch."

Khelani nodded. She was going to run to the rest room then get right to work. Time was money, and time was something that Khelani never wasted.

———

"WHAT CAN I GET FOR YOU?" The bartender at the restaurant that Anya was occupying walked over to her. It was only one in the afternoon, but she needed a drink, Badly.

"Let me get a double shot of Don Julio and a splash of pineapple juice. Also, I want to go ahead and order my food. I want the wings fried hard, a side of fries, and ranch."

"Coming right up."

Anya let out a small breath and looked around the bar. To say she was pissed would be an understatement. Her father was rich as fuck. To cut her off would just be flat out cruel. How dare he want his pretty ass daughters to pump drugs like niggas? All Anya wanted to have to worry about was being the best dressed, prettiest, bitch walking the streets and living off her father's dime until she snatched a baller of her own. With her face and her body, Anya was a hot commodity among most dope boys, scammers, and legit niggas that came across her path. In North Carolina, she had quite a few heavy hitters on her team, and she was almost sad when she had to leave. Almost. Anya knew Atlanta would be a come up for real. She could see herself right now being wifed up by a rich ass rapper or athlete. When Khelani got the job at the record label, Anya damn near creamed her panties. She wanted to get into all the parties and dope events off her sister's name, and she could do the rest.

Kemp and Khelani wouldn't even let her have that though. Anya had been chilling, but it looked like she was going to have to get serious about landing a baller. She was too fine, and her pussy was too good for her to be walking around broke. The bartender came back with her drink, and Anya wasted no time picking the glass up. After placing the tiny brown straw between her heavily glossed lips, Anya took three long sips.

"I see I'm not the only person that likes to day drink during the week." A pretty light-skinned chick that was just as tall as Anya with just as much body sat down beside her. She may have been a tad bit thicker than Anya. The woman gave her Megan Thee Stallion vibes as far as her body type. Anya did a quick evaluation of the woman, and shorty looked like a boss bitch indeed. Or she could have just looked the part and been as broke as Anya.

"It's 5:00 somewhere," Anya replied and took another sip. She wasn't exactly the friendly type, but when ole girl removed a pair of $1,200 shades from her face and placed them on the bar, Anya decided this was the type of bitch that she needed to be running with.

"My type of bitch. I'm Camila." She removed the strap of her Chanel bag from her shoulder and placed the purse in her lap. When she looked over at Anya, her light brown eyes flickered a bit, and a smile graced her face.

This bitch is bad, and she looks paid, Anya thought to herself. *She for sure has to know where the ballers are.* "Hi, I'm Anya."

"Anya that's a pretty name. Fits your pretty ass perfect. You from the A?"

Before Anya could answer, the bartender came back over and took Camila's drink order, and Anya ordered another drink. She was feeling all warm and tingly inside and just that fast, her previous agitation had melted away.

"I'm not. I'm actually from Trinidad. I've been here for a month now. Just trying to get a feel for the city and shit. I don't know anyone here but my older sister, and she has a stick up her ass." Camila giggled.

"I'm dead ass. All she wants to do is work. Real independent type bitch but me? Shit, if God wanted me to work hard, he wouldn't have made me so pretty. I need a nigga to spoil me. Period."

"Yoooooo," Camila laughed. "On God you my type of bitch. I have a feeling we can be great friends. So, you not working?"

"Nope. I didn't need to, but I have to make something shake soon."

"What about that ass?" Camila eyed her as Anya's eyebrows dipped.

"Huh?"

"I own a strip club. It opens at 4 pm to cater to businessmen that might not want to have business meetings in traditional places. It also caters to dope boys and scammers that might want to see some tits at 4 in the evening rather than 4 in the morning. Business has been booming lately and your pretty ass, baby you can make some bread in that muhfucka. Might even meet the nigga that takes ya ass up out of there. Feel me?"

Anya's eyes lit up. "I feel you." She'd never considered stripping because she didn't have to. Kemp or her niggas always spoiled her, but a lot of bad bitches were old strippers that were now the girlfriends of rich niggas. The days of niggas not wanting to wife strippers were over. Men didn't care about that shit anymore.

Camila didn't look to be too much older than her, and she was a boss bitch with her own club. Anya was willing to bet her last dollar that it was a nigga that put Camila on.

"Where is the club at?" she inquired as she finished off her drink.

"About ten minutes from here. Rappers love that muhfucka. They come in at least five nights out the week blowing bags. So do the scammers and dope boys. I'm telling you. Yesterday, four white corporate niggas were in there running up a check with black cards."

Anya felt all tingly inside, and she knew it wasn't just from the liquor. "Say less. When can I start?"

Camila smiled wide. "You can start tonight baby." She pulled out her phone. "What's your number? I'll text you all the details."

The drinks came along with Anya's food, and her and Camila laughed, drank, and conversed for an hour. By the time they were ready to part ways, Camila paid Anya's tab and when they did separate, Anya peeped Camila getting into a cocaine white Maserati.

"Oh, I can fuck with that bitch fa sho'," she admired as she headed to her black Jeep. "I'm 'bout to run this muhfuckin' money up and show my dad, I don't need his help," Anya smiled to herself.

Growing up in Trinidad, Anya hated it. Because her father was such a powerful man, she never had any privacy. She couldn't ride the bus to school with her friends, her father's driver took her. Even when her parents weren't home, there was always someone there be it a maid or a chef. Sneaking boys in was impossible, and Anya couldn't be the wild carefree teenager that she wanted to be. Even though she was spoiled, she often felt like she was in prison, and she hated it. When her father asked her and Anya to come to the states, Anya jumped at the chance, and she didn't care what the requirements were. She'd been able to bullshit her way through North Carolina, but Kemp was finally tired of her shit.

However now, things were looking up for Anya. She didn't view stripping as a real job. She'd be able to turn up on a nightly basis and get paid for it. That was right up her alley. It was a given that Kemp would be furious, but Anya didn't care. If she was taking care of herself there wasn't shit he could say, and he couldn't make her go back to Trinidad.

Chapter Three

"Yeah, I'm just now walking in my hotel room," Mozzy said, using his foot to close the door behind him.

He had his iPhone in one hand, on speaker phone, and his suitcase was in the opposite hand. He walked further into the penthouse suite and placed his bag down on the floor beside him. Mozzy looked around and smiled to himself. He was feeling the layout and it was a whole lot more lavish than what he was used to back in Houston. Mozzy knew right then and there that Atlanta was going to be good to him. The air smelled different and the money was looking a lot longer.

"I can't believe Big Man got you all the way out there," Judah, his cousin, said on the other end of the phone.

"I can't either. I was skeptical about coming to unknown territory, but I can fuck with this shit. Working for a nigga that has a record label and moves that work could be the kind of come up I need in my life."

"Damn right it is my nigga. You coming home off a bid. To have this kind of set up waiting on you is a blessing. You lucky as hell. Nigga, you were about to go down for a long ass time for a murder you didn't even do."

"That's how that shit goes man. Them motherfuckers don't give a fuck as long as they can close the damn case. I've been out for a few months though and I still haven't seen any real money like before I got locked up. Hopefully, this shit will change all of that. If I like the way shit is going, I may set up shop here."

"I don't see how shit can go wrong."

"I hope that's the case, but no matter how sweet shit looks, it can always go wrong. I have to get going. I'm supposed to be meeting Kyrie in about fifteen minutes, but I'm only ten minutes away."

"I heard that Atlanta traffic is a whole different ball game, so you might want to double the time."

"I'm 'bout to head that way. I'll hit you later."

"Aight."

Mozzy took a moment to look around the suite and take in his surroundings before he slid his phone in his pocket and headed back out of the room and down to the garage where his rental was. His current accommodations were very different from the cell he'd called home for more than a year. Kyrie had gotten him a suite and a rental. Mozzy couldn't wait to see what else came along with the job. Back in Houston before he got knocked, he had worked for a hustler by the name of Big Man. Mozzy had gotten locked up when he was twenty-two for murder. A murder that he didn't commit. Money had been good when he was on the streets, but it wasn't good enough for him to be able to afford the kind of lawyer that could get his case thrown out. Being innocent didn't mean shit. All the DA had to do was convince the jury that Mozzy had done it, and he was as good as sent up the river. Big Man believed in him though, and for that, Mozzy was eternally grateful. He sat in jail for over two years but when he finally went to trial, the lawyer Big Man hired showed why he was worth the $500 an hour that he charged.

Everyone had encouraged him to sue the police station that locked him up, but after everything that happened Mozzy wasn't fucking with the police at all. Plus, he may not have committed *that* murder, but he'd done plenty dirt. As he sat in his cell day in and day out, he felt that karma had come to pay his ass a visit for all the wrongs he did in the past. When he was finally freed, he tried the straight path for two weeks and was right back in the streets. He knew that didn't make any sense, but he had to live, and he didn't know anyone that would be eager to give him a job.

Even though Mozzy was glad to be free from the belly of the beast, he came home not knowing how he was going to get back on his feet. He'd already never be able to pay Big Man back for the lawyer, so he didn't want to ask the man to front him any work, but once again Big Man came through like his personal savior. Apparently Big Man's cousin had his hands full and he needed an unknown face to come in and help him out with some things. Mozzy didn't know exactly what he was going to have to do, but he was down for putting some money in his pockets. He finally made it to the garage and then hopped in his whip before pulling off to go find Kyrie's office building.

Exactly twenty minutes later he was pulling up to his destination and parking after getting lucky by spotting a car pulling out of a space that was fairly close to the entrance of the building. Mozzy got out of his car and rushed inside knowing that he was already a few minutes late.

"Excuse me," he said, walking up to the front desk and a red-haired woman held up a finger as she talked on the phone. Mozzy tapped his foot and looked down at his watch. It was five on the dot and he was trying to catch Kyrie before he left.

He knew Kyrie was expecting him, but Big Man had also told him that Kyrie waited for no one. "I need to speak with Kyrie," Mozzy said, rudely.

"Sir, just a minute." The woman pursed her lips

"Hell nah, you hold on. I got a meeting with Kyrie."

"Are you on the schedule to speak with Mr. Richmond?" she asked, pulling the phone away from her ear.

"I don't know shit about no schedule, but the nigga expecting me," Mozzy said, making the woman's eyes widen from his audacity. At the same time a guy with long dreads braided to the back spotted him and rushed over.

"I got this, Carey," he said and then directed Mozzy away from the front desk.

"Mozzy?"

"Yeah, how you know and who the hell are you?"

"I'm Ghalen, Kyrie's accountant and right-hand man. Little rough around the edges I see. You're about to be making a shit load of money so when you come into the office, I'd tone down the street shit. Though, you won't be here much this label is Kyrie's business. He keeps this and street shit separate, so all that hoodlum shit gotta go."

"Shit, I didn't know y'all niggas was doing it like this around this bitch. Niggas wearing suits and all," Mozzy stated amazed. He wasn't even offended at how Ghalen had checked him. All he knew was hood shit, but that legit paper was looking good as fuck.

"People that are serious about their business act accordingly. Kyrie doesn't require us to wear suits, but I'm a fly muhfucka and I dress as such," Ghalen chuckled. "I'll show you to Kyrie's office."

As they headed towards the elevator, he saw the secretary scowling, and he almost threw up his middle finger, but he had to remember where he was. This record label shit wasn't just a front. Kyrie was legit as fuck. When they reached the third floor, Mozzy followed Ghalen. Mozzy took in the hustle and bustle of the office before they stopped in front of Kyrie's door.

"Image," Ghalen spoke and winked, before heading back to the elevator, and Mozzy just shook his head and knocked on the door.

Mozzy was 6'1 with skin the color of a new penny, and he rocked a low fade. He was tall and muscular from all the weights he had lifted while he was locked up. Once he came home, he kept the workout regime up. He had grills in his mouth and everything about him screamed thug. That was mainly because of the two tear drops that were tatted right under his left eye and the fact that he kept an expression on his face like he was two seconds away from killing a nigga. He already knew he didn't fit in, and he hoped Ghalen was right. While all that Kyrie had going on was quite impressive, he would rather be in the streets putting his work in. Mozzy didn't want to have to be constantly worried about doing or saying the wrong things and feeling out of place.

"Come in."

Mozzy opened the door and stepped inside. He didn't even try to hide the fact that he was further impressed. Kyrie's office was spacious with floor to ceiling windows and decorated like some something out of a magazine.

"This shit is nice," Mozzy said, sitting in the white leather chair in front of Kyrie's desk. There was a matching couch tucked away in the corner with black pillows on it. Most of the office décor was black.

"Thank you. I had to make it comfortable because I spend a lot of time here. I'm glad you could make it though. Did my cousin run shit down to you or did he just send you out here blind?"

"Nah, he told me you needed help with some shit. I didn't know you was doing it like this though."

"Don't let any of this faze you. The business side of shit is just as crucial as the streets especially with the shit that goes on behind the scenes. Don't worry about all of that though. What do you say we hit the strip club tonight and we'll talk more then? I just wanted to see your face and see what was up with you. Ya' feel me?"

"Hell yeah, that's understandable. I'm down though, ain't shit like watching some naked hoes and discussing business."

"Exactly, I'll send you the time and address."

"Okay, cool," Mozzy said, standing up. He slapped hands with Kyrie once again and then made his way out of his office. He may not have known how big Kyrie was doing it at first, but after seeing everything Kyrie had going on, he was trying to be doing it big just like him one day. No matter how he had to get there.

KYRIE SLOUCHED DOWN and got comfortable in his seat as he cruised down the streets, of a suburban community, pushing his brand new Rolls Royce that he had paid a pretty penny to be customized. The outside was snow white and the inside was charcoal black. It had all of the latest features and he was blasting Jay-Z's classic album *Reasonable Doubt* through his Bluetooth system. Kyrie bobbed his head to the music as he made a right turn and then pulled in front of the house at the end of the street. He parked his car behind a matte black BMW Coupe and exited his vehicle.

He walked up on the porch and then knocked on the door. Work had passed by quickly and his day had already been pretty eventful. Kyrie wished he could have gone home and just called it a day, but he hadn't seen his folks in almost two weeks, so he knew he needed to show his face. Things had been busy for him lately, but his aunt and uncle would kill him if he didn't make time to check in with them. They had basically been raising him since he was fourteen and they looked at him like he was their own.

Kyrie's mother had died from Lupus related complications when he was fourteen, her brother made sure to become his father figure since he had never had one. He was a football coach at Kyrie's school and his wife was a nurse. He made sure to get Kyrie involved in football because he didn't want him hanging in the streets and continuing the lifestyle he had been living while his mother was alive. He lived in a nice neighborhood and he wanted Kyrie to turn over a new leaf. Losing a mother couldn't be easy, but losing a sister wasn't either and he was determined to make the best out of her child.

Therefore, Mario spent a lot of time with Kyrie on and off the field. When they weren't attending practice or a game they were in the gym. Mario tried to train Kyrie as much as he could while making sure he left time for Kyrie to worry about school. Since Kyrie was tied between the two Mario didn't think he would possibly have time to entertain the streets, but he didn't know his nephew as well as he thought he did at the time. Kyrie finished up high school and went off to college on an academic and athletic scholarship thanks to his uncle.

The truth didn't come out about Kyrie being involved in the streets until a year later when he got hurt on the field and lost his athletic scholarship. Since the pros were no longer in his future, he got involved in the streets a little deeper than he had been before, and the word got back to his uncle. Before, it was just hustling to have extra money and the latest fashions. After he got hurt, hustling became a way of life. Kyrie was ready to quit college and just come back home since that's where he had been spending the majority of his time at after losing his scholarship anyway. Mario refused to let him drop out though and told him just because he lost his athletic scholarship it didn't mean he lost his academic one. He told Kyrie to make his mother proud and finish school.

Kyrie wanted to do that, but he was also stubborn. He had already become addicted to the fast money, and he wasn't thrilled with the idea of graduating from college and going to slave for someone else's dream. He couldn't even be bothered to sit in a classroom all day and listen to professors lecture. Nah, he would keep hustling, stack his paper, and start his own business. Kyrie loved his uncle, but every last one of his speeches about the streets fell on deaf ears. Mario was just as stubborn as his nephew, and a part of him wanted to lay down the law. Disown Kyrie, threaten to cut him off, all that, but he couldn't. Life was short, and he already lost a sister. He couldn't stand the thought of not being in his nephew's life and then one day, Kyrie being gone. He made it clear that he didn't condone Kyrie's lifestyle, but the boy was now grown and there wasn't a thing he could do about it except love him, give him advice, and pray for him.

It was a tough decision to make but the last thing he wanted was for Kyrie to keep going behind his back and that's why he went with the first option. What Kyrie didn't know was that his uncle was also involved in the streets. He didn't make a living from just being a coach, but that was the side he never wanted his nephew to find out about. Since Kyrie had already made his own way in the streets Mario figured it would be better to bring him in under him instead of allowing Kyrie to work for someone that would only care about the money he was spending and not his well-being. Mario taught his nephew the in's and out's of the game.

So, by the time Kyrie graduated college his uncle had

taught him things about the game that he didn't know, giving him the ultimate advantage. He left college book smart and street smart. Now Kyrie was running things and Mario would only step in when he needed to. He had retired as a football coach, but he would always be a street legend. There were also things that Kyrie hipped his uncle to. Mario always felt it was best to keep your focus in one area. Specialize in one kind of drug, but Kyrie didn't see it like that. There was a lot of money in weed, and there would always be money in coke. He didn't see why he should have to choose, so he sold both.

"What's up, auntie?" Kyrie asked as soon as the front door was pulled open.

"Hey baby, what you out here knocking for?" Candace asked, giving her nephew a big hug as he walked in the door.

"You know I have to knock before I come in."

"That's nonsense. You might not live here anymore but this is still your house," Candace said, closing the door behind him. She had on a white pair of scrubs and her hair was pulled back into a neat ponytail. Mario and Candace were both in their fifties, but they looked much younger.

"What's up, old man?" Kyrie asked, walking over to his uncle who was sitting on the couch watching the news.

"Nothing much, what's up stranger?" They slapped hands and then Kyrie took a seat in the recliner next to the couch.

"I just left the office. It's been busy this last week."

"I see that."

"Would you like something to drink, Ky?" Candace asked, getting ready to head out of the living room.

"Nah, I'm good auntie, but thank you though."

"Okay, I'm finishing up dinner so make sure you get a plate before you go."

"Aight," Kyrie said as she walked out. "Camila been by lately?"

"She stopped by here a few hours ago. I'm sure she's down at that damn strip club now."

"Y'all still being hard on her?"

"We're not being hard enough and that's the damn problem. Candace didn't want me getting her that strip club in the first place, but we both know how your cousin is."

"Yeah, you're right about that. Once she has her mind set on something, there's no changing the shit."

"Exactly, college wasn't what she wanted to do, and she wasn't about to be leeching off us for the rest of her life. So, I gave her what she wanted, which was to own her own business. I'm glad she finally started taking the shit seriously and realized that running a business isn't so easy. She's not like us, you know we're both natural hustlers."

"True enough, but Camila is smart so I'm pretty sure she has everything under control."

"Oh, she has it under control, but it's how she got it under control that concerns me. The last time I checked the place was about to be shut down because of the lack of business, and her spending money on herself before paying the bills, but now all of a sudden the shit is doing better than ever before."

"What, you wanted it to close or something?"

"I do now, but only because Candace is driving me crazy about opening the shit for her. She swears clubs are dangerous and Camila shouldn't be running one. You know she sits in here all day and watches the depressing ass news."

"You know Auntie is kind of dramatic, but niggas get shot at the mall and in school. It isn't really safe anywhere."

"I told her that plenty of times, but she still worries. I got Camila the club to help her. Not to be a headache to me. You're a man, so I can get you wanting to do everything on your own without a handout but Camila," Mario paused and shook his head. "One day, she wants to be a grown independent boss and the next, she's back to being spoiled with her hand out. Trust me when I tell you, I'm glad business turned around because it keeps her out of my pockets. It's just the way it may have turned around that has me concerned. Camila may think she's cool and shit because she dates dusty ass niggas that tote guns, but she's not 'bout that life with her spoiled sheltered ass."

"What you talking about?" Kyrie's eyebrows snapped together in confusion.

"I've been informed that Camila is pushing drugs out of the club. I swear you kids are my karma. I don't know how true it is, but I want you to find out and shut that shit down. You hear me?" Mario looked over at his nephew, and Kyrie could see the anger in his eyes. Mario would go to war with the whole city behind his daughter, but at his age he would rather not. He just wanted her to lay low and chill out.

"Yeah, I got you unk."

Kyrie was amazed at how much his uncle knew. Even as adults, it was hard for him and Camila to get anything over on Mario. His ear was to the streets hard.

"Good. Now go get your uncle a beer." Mario laid his head back on the chair and placed his hands over his protruding belly.

Kyrie just shook his head and got up to go to the kitchen. His uncle's house was nice and in the suburbs, but it was nowhere near as nice as what he really could have afforded. The thing about Mario was, he had never been the flashy type. He did a short stint in the streets, and he felt that if he kept a low enough profile that he wouldn't entice his nephew to follow in his footsteps nor would he bring attention to himself. The money he made from coaching football was barely enough to pay the monthly bills and take care of his wife's car payment, car insurance, etc. Yes, she was a nurse, and she had her own bread, but Mario was old school. He prided himself on being a provider, so what his job didn't pay for, he used the money he made in the streets. His wife, used her money to do what she pleased, and she loved nice things, so it was nothing for her to have new furniture delivered or to take a nice lil' girl's trip with her sisters. Still, their life wasn't so flashy that Mario made himself look suspicious to anyone. In the eyes of those that didn't know him, he was just a simple man that liked working with kids, and he was middle-class. The money that he now lived off was from his days of stacking drug money and since he was so modest with his spending, it would last him for a minute. When it ran out, his wife assured him that she would hold him down when she retired from the hospital in a few years. Her 401k was already at almost $300,000 and still growing.

"Here you go," Kyrie said, walking back into the living room after he had got a beer for himself and his uncle.

He chilled for a couple of more hours and, he ate before heading home. An hour later he had showered and got fresh before heading right back out the door. Kyrie's days were often busy, and he didn't get much sleep, but that's what came along with running a company and the streets. Kyrie was hoping that with the extra help he brought in that he would start having time for himself. He had been working nonstop and a break was something that he could use. With everything going on in Uptown he wasn't so sure if he would ever get one. He finally pulled up to his destination and that's when his phone started ringing from the cupholder.

"Yooo?" he answered, after he had picked his phone up.

"What's up? Where you at?" Ghalen asked.

"I just pulled up at the strip club. I needed to come a little early and check shit out. I take it you're not coming?"

"Nah, Taylin tripping on a nigga." Ghalen sucked his teeth.

He was the same age as Kyrie, but he had been with his

baby mama Taylin for a while. They had their only son, Tamir, when they were sixteen and they had only been talking for a few months then, but their son had tied them together for life. They often bumped heads over shit like this, but Kyrie knew the two of them would be together forever. They were just crazy in love and the both of them stayed showing out. At work, Ghalen was well put together, but off the clock it was a whole different story.

"Damn, well if wifey said you can't come, then yo' ass can't come." Kyrie laughed.

"Shut up, you were the one who invited me out, so she's mad at you too."

"Man, tell Tay to stop that shit. She knows everything is business with us."

"That's the same shit I be telling her, but every time I say it, I'm a lying ass nigga."

"I ain't got shit to do with that." Kyrie chuckled.

"I was calling to let you know I wasn't gone make it though."

"Aight pussy whipped ass nigga," he joked before ending the call.

Kyrie opened his car door and then got out. He walked past the bouncer and gave him a head nod before proceeding inside of the club. The music was jumping, and Kyrie could feel the bass from the music. There were a few people sitting around the bar and a couple of guys were watching a stripper dance while barely throwing any money. It was still early so Kyrie knew the majority of the people wouldn't start pouring in until after one in the morning.

He walked straight through club and then went upstairs to where the office was located. He tapped on the door and then opened it and walked inside before anyone responded. When he walked in, he saw Camila sitting at her desk by the door, going off on somebody on her phone. She was wearing a pair of black leather leggings that look like they had been painted on with a black bra-top that Kyrie assumed was meant to be a shirt. She had on a pair of six inch heels, and Kyrie could only shake his head. Camila was going to always stand out and be well put together. One time he went to visit her when she had the flu, and even with a pale face, weak body, and a fever, she had lashes on, lip gloss coated her lips, and her bonnet matched her pajamas.

He walked over to the window and peeped through the blinds. The view overlooked the parking lot, and he could see a few people coming inside. Kyrie continued to watch for a few more seconds before closing them back and turning around to face Camila. She ended her phone call and then stood up. She walked over to Kyrie and gave him a big hug before stepping back.

"Hey what's going on?"

"Just came to check you out. Can you breathe in those damn leggings? I can already see somebody mistaking your ass for one of these strippers and then I'mma have to body me a muhfucka."

"The perks of having a big brother," Camila said, sarcastically. "Since when have you seen strippers walking around in leggings? I swear you and daddy stay reaching. Y'all about as dramatic as my mother," she rolled her eyes upwards.

Kyrie frowned "I'm a whole ass man. There ain't shit dramatic about me. I leave that to females. You got that bread for me?"

"Yeah, the money is in the safe. Just make sure you get it before you leave tonight."

"Bet. But your dad is up on game. I swear we be underestimating his reach in the streets. We got a good lil' thing going on here, but I can't let him find out I'm the one supplying you. We might have to wrap this shit up sooner than expected."

"See, I hate when you start talking like that. Don't even think about cutting me out the loop, Kyrie! My parents won't find out a thing. I just wish they'd let me grow the fuck up. Dang!" Camila stomped her foot like an oversized child.

"They were bitching when I wasn't making money and now that I am making money, they're still not happy."

"Your parents just want you safe Camila. You know that. They don't want to see you in jail or worse."

"But they don't say shit to you."

"Shawty I got plenty of lectures that you weren't around to hear. Uncle Mario didn't want me in the streets either, but it's a bit different with me. For one, I'm a man and right or not, there is a double standard."

Camila rolled her eyes. "Yeah whatever. All I'm saying is let me stack some bread first before you try to call shit quits. I'm hoping that I can get money coming in the right way too. I just hired a pretty ass new stripper, and she has a body to die for. You should meet her."

"I'm not interested, but I was sticking around anyway. I'm meeting with someone so just come find me in the VIP section if you need me."

"Okay, bruh," Camila said and then gave him another hug before he walked out.

By the time Kyrie made it back down to the club area Mozzy was walking through the door. Kyrie walked over and slapped hands with him before leading him up to the VIP section. Kyrie stopped one of the bottle girls and ordered them a bottle before he took a seat on the comfortable couch. The place was already starting to get packed and it hadn't even hit twelve yet. That was a good sign and that's why he knew his cousin would be okay without all of the extra shit.

She seemed to get a thrill out of danger though and she always had for as long as he could remember. So, he knew it wasn't going to be easy getting her to go back legit. If he could he'd kick his own ass for even asking her to help him wash his dirty money to begin with. He had started making more money out in the streets than he could wash through his own business and that's when he turned to Camila who was eager to help.

Since she was willing to help him, he didn't have a choice but to return the favor last year when she came crying to him about her place possibly being shut down because of the lack of business. She may have washed his money, but that didn't make it hers. Even though Kyrie had given her permission to use what she needed to keep her business afloat. When he started supplying her with drugs to sell in the club, she started getting a lot more customers and now that she was seeing all the business she was getting because of the drugs, stopping wasn't her goal anytime soon.

"Damn, this shit nice. You know the owner? I saw you coming from the back when I was walking in," Mozzy said, sitting a few spaces down on the couch.

"Yeah, my cousin owns the shit. What's good with you though?" Kyrie pulled a pack of cigars out of his pocket and then pulled out a blunt that was already rolled.

"I'm just ready to get to this money."

"I know that shit right," Kyrie said, sparking the blunt. "I just basically need you to be ready. At all times. Stay ready and you won't have to get ready. Anything I need handled, when I call you, I need you to be on it. We'll start out small and move up as I see fit."

Mozzy nodded. He was no stranger to the game, and he knew that Kyrie would need to feel him out first. Test him. He didn't have a problem with that.

"Aye, that's what I'm here for. Just say the word, and I got you."

The bottle girl finally came back up to their section and placed two bottles of Hennessy down in front of them. Kyrie tipped her and then she smiled at him before walking away. Kyrie poured himself a drink and passed his blunt over to Mozzy. The DJ was playing nothing but hits from mad Atlanta artists, and the place was now packed to capacity. The vibe was lit, and Kyrie was just chilling and enjoying his night while trying to feel Mozzy out a little bit.

The new stripper his cousin had been talking about was finally about to perform. All of the spotlights were on her as the song came on that she would be performing to. *Throat Baby* by BRS Kash came on, and Kyrie's eyes were trained on the dancer. He thought she was a pretty girl but, he could tell she probably wasn't his type. Kyrie had nothing against strippers, but he just liked a certain kind of woman. He wasn't judging, but he liked a woman that was on her shit that didn't have to use sex or her body to get there. As Kyrie narrowed his eyes, he thought about how much ole girl on the stage looked like Khelani. In fact, if it wasn't for the difference in their complexions, they could have passed for twins. He had only seen her in passing. He hadn't even had a chance to introduce himself, but he did peep that she was gorgeous indeed.

Kyrie thought Khelani was beautiful and he wanted to get to know her more since they would be working closely together. He didn't get to where he was by not being a smart businessman, and he knew it might not be smart to start anything personal with her. It was tempting though as he thought back to how her ass looked in those black slacks. She was quiet and professional, and he could dig that. Plenty a hood rat had come to the office dressed nice trying to get a job because their mission was to land a baller. Kyrie had learned to be real careful when it came to who he hired. His last administrative assistant had a degree in business, but she was as ratchet as they came, and she had a nothing ass baby daddy that she let drag her down into the gutter with him.

When she wasn't spending her time on the clock on the phone cursing him out, she was always needing to leave work early for some crazy reason. The only reason Kyrie had allowed her to stay around so long was because he had gotten used to her. When she did focus on the job, she did a damn good job of keeping shit running smoothly. However the final straw had been when her baby daddy came to the office and pulled a gun out on her because he thought she was fucking someone in the office. Kyrie hated to let her go, but that shit was bad for business and he was no longer able to deal with her shit.

"Hey bruh, you alright up here?" Camila asked a few minutes later and Kyrie looked over. He hadn't even noticed her walking up to the VIP section. She wasn't alone, however. She had the new girl in tow, and Kyrie noticed her gray eyes immediately.

"Yeah, I'm chilling." He had a slight buzz going on and was about ready to take it in for the night.

"Cool, I just wanted to bring Anya up here to meet y'all. This is my new money maker. She wasn't even dancing like this was her first time, was she?" Camila smiled gassing Anya up.

"First performance? Damn, I couldn't even tell. Baby, you were working the fuck out that pole." Mozzy looked over at Anya and licked his lips.

"See, I told you your ass killed that shit," Camila said, excitedly. She knew Anya had a lot of potential and she had already made a shitload of money her first night on the stage.

"I didn't know if you were just boosting my head or not. Thank you, sweetheart," Anya said, looking at Mozzy.

"I know we just met today, but if you haven't noticed yet, I don't sugar coat shit. Bitch you is bad on that stage!" Camila snapped, making Anya giggle. She then turned her attention to Mozzy who was damn near eye fucking Anya.

"Oh, I'm sorry I didn't even introduce myself. I'm Camila, Kyrie's people."

"Nice to meet you. I'm Mozzy." Mozzy was tipsy but not enough to be disrespectful. He wasn't about to eye fuck his boss' people. He would just focus on fine ass Anya. Mozzy licked his lips and bit his bottom lip as he zeroed in on Anya's pussy print.

Camila peeped the thirst in Mozzy's eyes. "I just wanted to say hello. You guys have fun and be safe." Camila looked at Anya and winked. "Go get them table dances girl."

"Come here, let me get a good look at you," Mozzy licked his lips again, and Anya sauntered over to him. He was all up in a section and had his own bottle of henny, so he must have had some paper, Anya assumed. She didn't know Kyrie paid for the bottles and the section was on the house.

Dressed in a black thong and matching bra, with clear six inch stilettos on, she stood in front of Mozzy and he grabbed her hand and made her do a little twirl so he could take all of her in. Her thighs jiggled like Jell-O and he just knew her ass was talking to him. Her titties were sticking out the top off her top and he was ready to French kiss them and wear Anya's ass out in the bedroom. He didn't even take into consideration that he really didn't have money to spare for a dance. Mozzy pulled her down on his lap and she turned around and smiled at him.

"You sexy as fuck, but you already know that, huh?" he whispered to Anya, his breath tickling her ear. She had a regular ear piercing and an industrial piercing at the top.

"It wouldn't be my first time hearing it." Anya smiled. Flirting was her thing, so this job was right up her alley.

"And it damn sure won't be your last." All of his reservations about spending went out the window when she started gyrating on his lap to the Lil' Baby song that was playing.

Kyrie got up in preparation to make his exit. Anya was exactly the type of female he had suspected her to be. She was just another bitch fucking and sucking for her next pair of Louboutin heels. He loved a woman on her shit, but there were more ways to get things than spreading legs for them. There were the strippers that just danced. They didn't fuck men from the club or sell pussy. Kyrie knew right away that Anya was the anything goes type.

He picked up his bottle of henny and took a few more swallows. He knew he couldn't finish a pint to the head, but purchasing the bottle was business for the club. He didn't care about what got left in the bottle. Damn near every person he passed attempted to stop him and speak, but Kyrie simply gave a head nod and kept it moving. Once he was in the back, he made his way back up the stairs and went into his cousin's office. He walked over to the closet and then opened the door with a kiss of his teeth before kneeling down to put the code in the safe that was inside of the closet. He had told Camila about not having the door locked. That was that careless shit that he hated dealing with. At times, running some shit with her felt more like babysitting than a partnership.

"You about to head out?" Camila asked, walking in the office.

"Yes and keep this fucking closet door locked. What do I keep telling you about this shit?"

"Okay, Ky. I hear you." Camila rolled her eyes. "Who was that guy you were sitting with in V.I.P.?" Camila asked as Kyrie got ready to walk out.

"Just a nigga Big Man sent to town to help me out with some shit."

"And you trust him?"

"I don't know him. That's why I have to feel him out. Why? You know something I don't?"

Camila shrugged. "I'm just saying he has that money hungry look in his eyes. I know it when I see it and he definitely has it."

"That could be a good thing for me as long as he doesn't get the bright idea to try and cross me but these days, that's a chance you take with anybody. I got this," Kyrie assured her.

"I hear you. So, you weren't interested in Anya at all? She's beautiful and the bitch has body for days."

"Nah, I told you I wasn't interested off top."

"That was before you even saw her. For as long as I've known you, I've never seen you with anyone. I know you have trust issues, but I was just trying to help."

Kyrie chuckled, "Baby girl when I'm ready to fuck with somebody, she for damn sure has to have more than a pretty face and a nice body. Atlanta is full of superficial, cappin' ass, wanna be YouTube stars and IG models, build a body females that's good for pussy and head. That's it."

Camila shook her head. "Don't act like the A isn't full of some boss bitches too."

"You're right, and I want a boss bitch that didn't become a boss from selling pussy."

"Whatever Kyrie. Goodnight." Camila tried not to be too offended by his words, but she was damn near what he described. She wasn't a stripper, but she would give her pussy up to the highest bidder. And she didn't see a damn thing wrong with it.

Chapter Four

"And where have you been?" Khelani asked Anya as she peered over the red coffee mug that was resting against her plump lips. It was almost six in the morning, and Khelani had to be at work in three hours. She needed enough time to go get some weed and give it to Kasim so he could make a move for her. Khelani was exhausted and glad the next day was Saturday, so she could sleep in. She kept telling herself that there was no money in sleeping, but her body was tired. She didn't have a life outside of hustling. Grabbing work was shit that Anya could have been doing to help her, and Khelani was starting to resent her sister more and more.

Anya's eyes were barely open, but she managed to roll them. She was drunk as hell and high as fuck and not in the mood to be questioned by her sister. Khelani stood in the kitchen dressed in a red pencil skirt, a black and white polka dot blouse, and grey house slippers. Her curls were popping, and she looked like a damn librarian. A cute librarian, but she still looked like one and that made Anya frown.

"Work," she snapped and opened the fridge for some juice.

Khelani jerked her head back. "Work? Where in the hell do you work?"

Anya smirked. "A strip club."

Khelani peered at her sister with her mouth agape and waited for her to give an indication that she was joking. When she saw that Anya appeared to be serious, she placed her cup on the counter.

"Are you trying to make dad come snatch your ass up?"

"I am grown!" Anya shouted. "He already cut me off. What more can he do? I don't want to sell drugs. I just don't. I'll move out and get my own place. Tell him to send someone else over here to help you and Kasim. You and him both can stop threatening me. I don't care anymore Khelani. I'll be out of here in a few days."

Khelani just stared after her sister as she walked away. Life was going to have to kick Anya in the ass a few times before she grew the fuck up. Their mother spoiled her, and Khelani often made excuses for her. Khelani loved Anya to death, but Anya couldn't be her problem anymore. If she wanted to be grown, then she could go be grown. Anya wouldn't always have the luxury of having someone to clean up her messes and at that moment, Khelani was done. Anya could move out, she could strip, she could defy their father, she could do whatever it was that she felt she needed to do. Khelani finished her coffee and went to put her shoes on. She had to go handle her business. Time spent thinking about Anya's bullshit was time she didn't have.

Once she reached her destination, Khelani's eyes scanned the sixty pounds of weed that sat before her. Once she was sure that every pound was accounted for, she grabbed ten and placed them in a black duffel bag. The pounds were in bubble wrap and saran wrap, so their potent smell didn't overpower the air. Once the duffel bag was zipped up, she closed the safe back and exited the room. She handed the bag to Kasim.

"I don't wish to sit on the phone half the morning with my father and answer questions about Anya. Call him and tell him he needs to send more help. I'm giving this job at least another five weeks, and I'm tired already. I won't ask you to help me alone. Since Anya isn't pulling her weight, one more person should help."

Kasim nodded. "Got it."

He had known Kemp for more than twenty years. Ten years before, Kasim's wife died from breast cancer. They never had children, and when she died, he was left all alone. His mother had also lost her fight with cancer when he was nineteen, and Kasim was bitter with life. He was angry, and he had no desire to get close to anyone else. With no one at home, he threw himself into work. He proved himself time and time again and became one of Kemp's most loyal and trusted workers. For Kasim going with the girls to the states and keeping them safe, was an honor and he was paid handsomely. Kemp sent him $10,000 a month for his bills and personal money. He also sent Kasim money to purchase the black Escalade that he drove the girls around in. Kasim was nothing more than a glorified baby-sitter, but he didn't mind. Not for what he was getting paid. His bills and living expenses barely came to $2,000 a month. That left him with around $8,000 a month to do with what he pleased.

He knew just like Kemp that Khelani was the smart one. Anya was a rebel and had more than likely given Kemp a few gray hairs. Kasim got paid to do a job, but he didn't necessarily agree with Kemp. He should have sent a nephew or a male cousin to take over the states. Not his daughters. Khelani was headstrong, and she was damn near the male version of Kemp, but she was still a woman. In Kasim's eyes, she didn't need to be risking her life or her freedom to be a queen pen. She should be somewhere getting married and making babies, but she had no interest in that. She was taking over various cities in various states and ensuring that Kemps empire continued to grow. And as long as she was doing that and he was breathing, Kasim would be by her side as her protector.

ONCE THAT WAS TAKEN care of, Khelani hopped in her car and headed to work. Khelani looked the part of an office worker. It was her second day at work, and she was wondering if she'd at least meet Kyrie. Many would kill for the $2,400 salary she was getting every two weeks, but that barely covered the rent on her condo. Khelani could make that in one day. She needed to figure out how to meet the people that she needed to meet. The ones that would buy weed by the pound. Several pounds at a time.

"You're too powerful. You know that right? No man will ever want to be with you because you'd steal his shine. You need to be softer. More submissive."

The words that Kasim spoke to Khelani played over and over in her mind. Most days, she loved being who she was. Khelani loved being strong, determined, smart. She'd seen other females laugh and giggle and play the role of a dumb bimbo just to stroke a man's ego, and she would never. She saw the women that broke their necks to chase behind niggas with a bag. She also would never. Khelani had her own bag, but she was a woman by nature. Sometimes, just once in a blue moon she wanted to be soft. She wanted to be dainty and not have to worry about running a drug empire. Anya was right about one thing. They'd never been given a choice. Khelani just always did what was expected of her. Whatever it took to make her parents happy, and she soon found it was easier to make her father happy than it was her mother. Her mother criticized everything, and nothing was ever good enough for her. Khelani could bust her ass only to be ridiculed, but Anya could throw together the bare minimum, and their mother would be elated.

She could relate to Anya when she complained about Khelani being her father's favorite. If Khelani ever had kids, she couldn't see herself having a favorite. But then again, she didn't have kids, so she didn't know what she'd do or wouldn't do. It just didn't seem fair. Once Khelani arrived at work, she parked her car, grabbed her things and headed inside. She ran into the elevator just before the doors could close, and she came face to face with a very handsome man. He was 6'4 with skin the color of melted caramel, and a thick full beard. His head held a mass of curls, and he had an athletic build. One like that of a football player. His cologne filled the air inside of the elevator, and he was dressed in black jeans that weren't too loose or too tight, a black button up shirt, and a pair of wheat colored Timberlands. He didn't look too street, and he wasn't really dressed up, but he didn't look out of place at all. If Khelani was looking for a man, her job would be the perfect place to find one because there wasn't a shortage of them at the record label.

"What floor?" the man in the elevator had a deep voice. A voice so deep that it made Khelani's pussy quiver. That was something powerful indeed. She had to squeeze her legs together to stop the sensation.

"Third. Thank you."

The stranger cocked his head slightly to the left. "Khelani right?"

Khelani turned her face towards his. "Yes. Khelani Touissant."

The man extended his hand for her to shake. "I'm Kyrie. The owner of the label."

Khelani wasn't sure what to expect with Kyrie, but she damn sure didn't expect for him to be that fine. She shook his hand and gave him a small smile. "It's a pleasure to meet you."

"Likewise. I've heard good things about you so far. Keep up the good work." The elevator stopped on the designated floor, and Kyrie tipped his head in her direction and stepped off.

Khelani was right behind him, and her eyebrows shot up as she headed towards her desk. The perks at the record label were looking better and better. She ruled out the thought of love long ago, but last year's fiasco in North Carolina had for sure reminded her that she was naïve as hell. She was naïve to think that happily ever after fairytale love bullshit was true. There were people that were happy and in love but in most instances, it was a façade. Khelani learned with her parents that what people often show the world is a different story than what goes on behind closed doors. She didn't have the desire nor the energy to fake any damn thing, and she had no desire to change who she was to get a man to claim he liked her, maybe even loved her, only to take her for granted.

Khelani gave a smile and a hello to those around her before sitting down to log into her computer. From what she knew, Kyrie wasn't only a successful businessman, he flooded most of Georgia and South Carolina with coke. He also dabbled in weed. From what she understood, he got the majority of the money from his coke. Khelani's plans were to eventually become the most sought after marijuana connect in Georgia, and Kyrie could do one of two things. He could either fall in line and start buying from her, or she would take his clientele, and there wouldn't be shit he could do about it.

After logging into her computer, Khelani got right to work. Being about her business came natural to her, so she worked diligently. Kasim knew not to bother her unless it was an absolute emergency, and she didn't have friends or a social media page. Her phone was on vibrate, and it wasn't a distraction. Khelani worked hard, and before she knew it, three hours had passed. Little did Khelani know, she was being watched by a lot of the people in the office, and they admired her hard work. To them, she didn't appear to have a motive. She didn't constantly ask questions about the rappers signed to the label, and she hadn't asked when any of the parties or events were. She was a breath of fresh air, but no one was watching her harder than Kyrie. Since being close to her in the elevator, all of his common sense went out the window. Sleeping with the employees would more than likely end up bad every time, but he wouldn't be him if he didn't at least attempt to get to know Khelani.

"Knock knock," Kim stuck her head in the door and said the words instead of actually knocking.

Kyrie tore his eyes away from the monitor on his desk. There were cameras in every room at his label, and he watched his employees regularly. Kim had been working for him the longest, and she knew him almost as well as he knew himself.

"Looking at the new girl?" she entered his office without being invited.

Kyrie smirked. "You think you know me."

"I do know you, nigga. Remember what happened last time," she sat down in front of him and crossed her legs.

Kyrie smiled and shook his head. "Nothing bad happened last time."

"Nothing except one of the damn cleaners became obsessed with you after you fucked her. You would go days without coming in just to avoid her."

Kyrie laughed at the memory. "But then she got pregnant by Sway, and I haven't seen the bitch since."

"Anyway, I won't be here tomorrow. My daughter has a

doctor's appointment, but I think Khelani can keep things running. She's a fast learner and about her business."

"So I've been hearing. Ghalen said the same thing. I think I'm going to invite her to Kobie's party tomorrow."

Kim's eyebrows hiked up. "Are you inviting her so she can get to know some of the artists on the label or for personal reasons?"

"I'm your boss shawty. You're not mine. Chill on the interrogation."

Kim put her hands up in surrender. "You got it boss. She's a hard worker, so don't mess this one up because you might be in charge but when the admin assistant slacks, it makes my job harder."

Kyrie kissed his teeth. "I got you damn. You don't have no faith in your boy."

"None at all," Kim was half-joking and half-serious as she stood up and walked away.

Kyrie picked up his phone and dialed Khelani's extension. He licked his lips when the melodic tone of her voice came through the speaker of the phone. "It's Kyrie. Can you pause whatever you're doing and step inside my office for a minute?"

"Sure. I'll be right there."

Kyrie sat back in his chair and waited for Khelani. "Come in," he called out after she knocked lightly on the door.

When Khelani entered the office, Kyrie's dick got harder than steel. He wasn't sure if it was the hair, her eyes, her curves, or what. He was so used to women with weave hanging down to their asses, that her natural hair was sexy as hell to him. Her nails were short and a nude color. Everything about her was classy and simple. Khelani was his definition of a bad bitch. She didn't have to do too much at all, and she could still gain a man's undivided attention. "Have a seat," he motioned his head towards the chair.

Khelani sat down, and Kyrie tried to read her. She looked confident and sure of herself. There wasn't the slightest hint of nervousness displayed. Kyrie found it odd that he was damn near lost on how to come at her.

"Tell me a little bit about yourself. What made you want to work for a record label?"

"I'm twenty-four, and I am from Trinidad. I've been in the states for two years, and I've only been in Atlanta for one month. I didn't necessarily set out to work at a record label, but when I read the job description, I felt that my experience and skills would be an asset to the label."

Her answer made Kyrie's dick even harder. There was nothing like a smart sexy chick.

"Word. Your resume is definitely impressive. What brought you to Atlanta?" his eyes scanned her finger to see if she was wearing a wedding ring.

"I love the fact that there are so many professional black people here."

"Indeed, there is. You have kids? A man? I ask because one of my artists, Kobie is having a party tomorrow night. All the artists on the label will be there. It will be a good way for you to meet everyone. We're like family around here."

I don't have kids, and I am single. My sister is the only person I know here, so a networking event will be nice. Just give me the information, and I'm there."

"I'll get your number off your resume and text you. Enjoy the rest of your day."

"Thank you."

Kyrie lustfully watched her as she walked out of his office. She was new in town and had only been in the states for two years. He wondered what her story was, but he didn't want her to feel like he was interrogating her, so he cut the Q&A session short. If she was single, there would be time to get to know her later. He already knew that the men at the party would be on her like dogs on meat. It was time for lunch, so Kyrie left the office to head down to one of his favorite restaurants. As he was heading towards his car in the parking garage, he saw Khelani getting into a burnt orange beamer.

"Got damn, and she got bread too? I need to find out what's up with her for real."

Kyrie's phone rang, breaking him from the trance that Khelani had him in. He saw that his homie Tae was calling. "What up?"

"Yo, we have a slight issue. Kenyatta didn't re-up this month, neither did Jimmy, or Vato. There seems to be a new connect in town with some fire ass weed."

Kyrie pinched the bridge of his nose. There a total of six dope ass rappers and singers signed to his label, and they were all making him money out the ass. He wasn't broke. The money he made from the label was what he paid his bills with, and there was often money left over even after he looked out for different people and spent money on dumb shit. The money he made from coke went into his retirement fund and the money he made from weed was his bullshit money. Like when he wanted to go to Dubai for five days or spend $120,000 on a watch. It for damn sure wouldn't cause him to run up on hard times because a few people didn't re-up, but that wasn't what he was trying to hear.

And who is this person?"

"I don't know yet. I'm trying to find out."

"Do that."

Kyrie ended the call and started his car with a scowl on his face. He was the man to see in Atlanta for weed, and he needed to know who was trying to step in on his territory so they could be handled accordingly.

Chapter Five

"What's this?" Anya asked Camila as she pulled into the parking lot of a white building. There was a sign on it that said *Cutz and Grillz*. As soon as Anya woke up for the day, Camila was texting her and asking her if she wanted to hang.

"My girl Caresha does hair in the front, and her nigga Snow does grills in the back. I have to come pick my shit up from him, but Caresha is one of the dopest stylists in the city, and she doesn't charge celebrity prices. You should check her out."

When Anya straightened her hair, it touched the middle of her back, so she didn't really see the need to spend a crazy amount of money on bundles. She had her own thick mane, but she did like to rock braids every few months. She got out of the car and followed Camila into the establishment. If she kept having nights at the club like her first night, she'd be able to move out of Khelani's condo and into her own place in no time. It was time to finally show her dad and sister that she was grown and could take care of herself. A nice ass one bedroom was attainable as long as she kept seeing good money from dancing.

When Anya and Camila entered the building, the first thing Anya noticed was that it was hood as hell. A pretty brown-skinned chick with a purple lace front on was standing behind a swivel chair doing a sew-in. There was one person under the dryer and another waiting.

"Hey boo," the girl with the purple hair spoke to Camila.

"Hey Love. This is my girl Anya. She's new in town, and I told her you do the best hair around."

"That I do," Caresha smiled.

Anya smiled back, but she could feel the other patrons of the shop eyeballing her. With her face and her body, she was used to glares from jealous bitches. She didn't care as long as nobody said anything to her.

"Snow back there? I have to pick my grill up."

Caresha rolled her eyes upwards. "Yeah his trifling ass is back there. Bitch ass nigga," she mumbled, and Camila chuckled.

"Y'all on that again? You hate him at least once a month, but neither one of y'all not going nowhere."

"Keep thinking that," Caresha stated with a suck of her teeth.

"Don't worry. I am." Camila started walking to the back, and Anya followed her.

When they reached the back, Anya peeped a brown-skinned dude with shoulder-length dreads. They were dyed blonde and ordinarily, she wouldn't care for a guy with dyed hair of any color, but Snow wasn't bad looking at all. He was a little short for her taste. He looked to be about 5'9, but he couldn't have everything. If his pockets were deep, that would make up for his height. For a second, Anya thought she was getting beside herself, but she didn't miss the way Snow looked at her before greeting Camila.

"What up? I was just about to text you. I got that all wrapped up for you."

"I can't wait to see them," Camila squealed while Anya looked around.

"How long would it take for me to get a bottom grill?" she inquired while looking at various pictures on the wall of grills that Snow had made.

"If you have time, I can do the mold now, and you can come back and get them tomorrow."

"Bet." Anya looked over at Camila. "We got time for that?"

"Sure."

Camila watched as Snow grabbed some gloves while Anya got comfortable in his chair. Snow was the average man. He would eye fuck any decent looking female and try to actually fuck most of them. Caresha had caught him in so much shit over the years it wasn't even funny. They had an intense history. Snow and Caresha met in middle school. He took her virginity at the age of fifteen, and they had been together off and on for the past eleven years. In that eleven years, they had three kids, and he'd given her four different STD's. The longest they ever stayed apart was four months, and Caresha had the time of her life being really single for the first time. She was having too much fun because when Snow caught wind of that shit, he damn near committed suicide. Camila didn't understand why Caresha put up with his shit, but she didn't need to. At the end of the day, Camila was her girl, and she had her back. That's why as soon as they were done and in her car, she put Anya up on game.

"That nigga Snow is gon' flirt with you. I bet my bottom dollar on that shit, but he's off limits. No matter what Camila says, her and Snow are locked in. Don't even mess with his ass."

Anya simply nodded. She wasn't going to throw herself at Snow, but if he came on to her, she just might see what he was talking about. She respected Camila's loyalty, but Caresha was her friend. Anya didn't know the bitch, and she said out of her own mouth that her and Snow were broken up. It had been over a month since Anya had some dick, and she was ready. Mozzy had been on her hard as hell when she gave him a lap dance, but she was on the fence about him. He was aight, but Snow looked way better.

Camila cut into Anya's thoughts. "My cousin, the one that was in VIP last night, he has a record label. One of his artists is having a party tomorrow. You trying to come?"

Anya looked over at her newfound friend with wide eyes. "Fuck yes I want to go! Shit, I need a new outfit. Wait, my sister works for a record label. I wonder if his is the one. What's his name again?"

"Kyrie Richmond."

'Yeap that's him,' Anya thought to herself. Small world. So, Camila's cousin was the plug and the person that Khelani was trying to get connections through.

"Sounds familiar. I have to ask her, but I'm in."

"Awesome. I'm telling you. Stick with me kid, and Atlanta will be good to you."

All Anya could do was smile because for some reason, she felt that this was true, and she was all for it.

THE NEXT DAY, Anya went to the mall and picked out an outfit that was sure to turn heads at the party. Since her father had cut her off and she knew Khelani wouldn't give her money, she had to use the money she made the night before, which was damn near a stack. Anya had a pair of black Gucci tights that would set the outfit off just right. They were see through with the G's on them. She was going to rock a pair of denim booty shorts, a black bra, and some strappy black heels. Anya could pull a man in sweats and a hoodie but to go to the club, she was putting all the goods she'd been blessed with on display. She needed to hit a lick. And in her mind, any sexy ass nigga with money was the lick she needed to come across. Honestly, he didn't even have to be sexy. An ugly nigga with deep pockets would do the trick too. A middle-aged white man was the person that purchased her, her first Fendi bag. Even though Anya came from money, a man still had to be on his shit to have sex with her. In her eyes, she was a princess and needed to be treated as such. And what better way to treat a princess than to spoil her relentlessly? She wasn't Khelani, and she wasn't working for a damn thing. Unless one counted her working that pole at Camila's club.

Anya was glad that when she went to get her grills from Snow, the hair salon portion of the shop was closed and empty. She knew whether Snow was single at the moment or not, if she pulled up without Camila while Caresha was there, all eyes and ears would have been on her.

"Hey," she greeted Snow as she entered the room and saw him perched on a stool, head down, scrolling through his phone.

He looked up and smiled at her. "What's good Baby Girl? I got your shit right here." He stood up, and Anya's eyes fell on his dick print in his grey sweatpants. It looked like he was working with a monster for sure.

"Good. I'm going to a party tonight, and I want to rock them."

"Oh yeah? That all you doing tonight?" Snow tossed Anya a curious glance.

She eyed him intently to look for a clue that he was flirting.

She didn't want to take his kindness and casual conversation to mean something more if he wasn't actually trying to get at her, but she could read the look in his eyes. Snow was flirting with her. "Is there something else that I need to be doing?"

Snow smirked and licked his lips. "I'll leave that up to you to decide. I'll probably be out tonight too. Take my number."

Anya bit her bottom lip and looked Snow up and down. He was dressed very casual and plain. Grey Polo sweats, a plain white tee that fit snug on his muscular frame. He was lean, but Anya could tell he worked out. Her eyes took in the veins that bulged down his arms and wondered if he had protruding veins in his dick. The only jewelry he wore was a watch. A lot of people rocked grills, but Anya couldn't look at Snow and surmise how much he was holding. Maybe he had money. Maybe he didn't. There was something about him though and even if he didn't have bread like that, maybe he could scratch her sexual itch until she found the baller to come along and scoop her.

"Nah it ain't gon' be that easy. You gon' have to call me and if I'm free, we might be able to link."

"I heard that." Snow unlocked his phone, and Anya rattled off her number to him.

She smiled even wider when he rang her up and gave her 50% off her grills. She definitely didn't want to spend all of her money. Especially since she was missing a night of work to go to the party with Camila, but she wasn't even mad. If she played her cards right, missing work would be worth it. After putting her grills in, Anya smiled at her reflection in the mirror. Yeah, she was that bitch for sure. After flirting with Snow for a few more minutes, Anya got in her car and headed home. Tonight, was going to be a movie, and she was excited as hell. When she pulled into the parking garage, she saw that Khelani was home, and she decided to ask her about the party. They hadn't been seeing much of each other lately, and Anya wondered if she was still mad at her. More than likely she was because Khelani could hold a damn grudge.

When Anya entered the condo, she saw Khelani standing at the island in the kitchen pulling a plastic bag containing a seafood boil out of a plastic bag. She was dressed in a grey robe, and her hair had been straightened and was pulled up into a high ponytail.

"Damn that smells good," Anya's stomach growled as the aroma from the food wafted into her nostrils. When Khelani didn't speak, Anya kissed her teeth. "Damn K you still mad? Get off that shit already. You know I love you, and me not helping was nothing personal against you."

Khelani untied the plastic bag and removed a shrimp. "Oh, you actually love someone other than yourself? Interesting."

"Really Khelani?" Anya's feelings were lowkey hurt. "Say I didn't help you in North Carolina. Say I didn't tell you that I didn't want to do it anymore time and time again. Say I didn't encourage you to let this shit go and give Malachi a chance when you started feeling him."

"Well that would have been the wrong thing to do. He would have robbed me blind and I would have defied dad for nothing."

"Okay so besides that. I get that some niggas aren't shit, but are you truly happy living like this? If you choose not to fall in love do it because that's what you want and not what dad is telling you. He can't dictate your life. Don't fall in love, choose the money. What? You don't want kids one day?"

"Anya none of that changes the fact that you've seen me running myself ragged working a job and hustling, and you never offered to help since we've been here. You just sleep and party and leave me to figure shit out on my own, but it's all good. Delante is coming over to help me and Kasim out."

"K please stop being mad at me. I'm sorry. I miss my sister. We are all we have here."

"Okay Anya whatever." Khelani pulled her corn on the cob from the bag and began eating it.

"So, the owner of the club that I dance at, Camila is Kyrie's cousin. We're going to some party tonight that he's throwing. How is it working for him?"

Khelani shrugged one shoulder. "It's a job, and it's serving its' purpose. I'll be at the party too. I haven't met any of the artists at work, so tonight will be my chance. It won't be tonight, but once I'm in good with a few of them, I'll ask them who they cop their weed from and ask them if they want to try my shit. No true smoker ever turns down the chance to taste different kinds of exotic weed."

"See! You have a good plan. It might not even take you six weeks at that job to gain the clientele that you need. Once a handful of people get their hands on that shit you're pumping, word of mouth will do the rest."

"Hope so."

Anya could tell Khelani still had a slight attitude, but she was softening up a bit. She was a natural hard ass but if she loved you, you'd know it. Anya walked over to the fridge to look for something to eat. Khelani's food smelled so good, she wished she had stopped and gotten something, but she wasn't going back out. Anya knew she had to put something on her stomach before she started drinking. Her and Khelani stayed on the go too much to ever spend a lot of time cooking, so there wasn't a lot to choose from. Anya quickly decided on a bacon, egg, and cheese sandwich, and she gathered the necessary ingredients. She playfully looked over at Khelani who was eating in silence.

"Dang, I know you're mad. You didn't even offer a nigga a shrimp."

A small smile graced Khelani's beautiful face. "You know I don't play 'bout my shrimp, but you can have a cluster of crab legs."

"Ohhh thank you." Anya's eyes lit up as she reached for the crab legs.

When she was done cooking and eating, Anya saw that it was almost ten, so she took a shot of Don Julio and went to take a shower. She blasted her music and an hour and a half later, she was dressed and make-up done. She entered the kitchen and saw Khelani standing in the living room scrolling through her phone.

"Sis you look amazing!" Anya gushed, and she wasn't exaggerating either. It had been a long time since she'd seen Khelani dress up in something other than work clothes. She hated how her sister was so all about business and never let her hair down. She loved money too but damn, what good was having the money if you never took time off to enjoy it?

Khelani was dressed in a nude bodycon dress that looked painted on. The dress clung to every curve of her body like it had been tailored just to fit her. On her feet, were peep toe black platform heels, and her hair hung down past her shoulders.

"Thank you," she replied to her sister. "My uber is almost here."

"Wait! You have to take a shot with me." Khelani ran over to the island and poured Khelani some tequila in a shot glass. She was going to drink hers straight from the bottle.

Khelani did want to let her hair down a bit and have some fun, so she grabbed the glass without protesting and tossed it back. She scrunched up her face as the harsh liquid made its' way down her throat.

"Okay I have to go. He's a minute away, and you know sometimes the elevator is slow."

"Byeeeee sissy." Anya was feeling good off her two shots, and she took another one. Her phone chimed, and she ran to her room to get it. Seeing a text from Camila that she was on the way made Anya smile.

By the time she put gloss on her lips, heels on her feet, and sprayed some perfume, Camila had arrived. When Anya got in the car, the smell of weed smacked her in the face.

"Okay you smoking that premium gas," Anya declared.

"And that's all I smoke." Camila passed her the blunt, and the women danced in their seats and turned up all the way to the club.

Anya was on a mission. She had Snow in her back pocket when she wanted dick, now she needed a money man. She didn't come to the A to play, and it was time for her to leave her mark.

Chapter Six

"Nigga said he got it from a bitch," Tae informed Kyrie as they sat in the back of his Bentley. Kyrie had a whole fleet of cars. Six to be exact, and he kept a driver on standby for occasions like these.

Tonight, was a celebration, and he had already kicked it off. He sat in the back of the luxury car with a bottle of Belaire in one hand and a fat ass blunt in the other.

"A bitch?" he frowned up his face before placing the blunt between his lips and taking a deep pull. "What's her name?" his voice came out choppy as the smoke left his lungs.

"Kenyatta claimed that she just told him that he could deal directly with a nigga named Kasim, but he knew she was running shit."

The scowl on Kyrie's face deepened. "How you do business with a bitch and you don't even know her name?"

Tae shrugged. "He just said she was a pretty ass bitch. Not from around here, and he could tell she was on some boss type shit. Said her weed is like that. Shorty got some mochi, gelato, and some other kind of weed. Platinum skunk or some shit."

Kyrie kissed his teeth in agitation. "So, this nigga was so mesmerized by the bitch's beauty that he didn't even ask her name? Ain't no fuckin' way. What if her ass is the law? Is her being pretty gonna save his dumb ass?"

Tae shrugged. "I'm just the messenger. If her weed is potent like that, we'll find out how to get in touch with her soon enough."

Kyrie hit the blunt feverishly to keep his agitation at bay. It was supposed to be a night of fun. He had accomplished a lot and had several multi-millionaires signed to his label. If he was being honest with himself, Kyrie knew that it was his ego that had him tripping about this new weed supplier. He didn't *need* the money he was missing, but he certainly wanted it. Of course, he wasn't the only person in the A that sold weed, but he was still pissed that someone came in and took several of his customers away at once. What if more followed?

As his driver pulled up in front of the club, Kyrie placed the bottle of champagne to his lips and took a swig. Fuck all that. It was time to celebrate. He put the bottle down and exited the car. As he stood on the sidewalk and waited for Tae, he saw Khelani walking towards the entrance, and his dick reacted as it normally did when he saw her. The effect that she had on his manhood was crazy. He peeped that she was alone, and he eyed her through hooded lids.

"I'm glad you could make it," he stated stepping closer to her. He saw some niggas turn around and stare at her ass. Just as he'd predicted. Men would be on her all night unless he kept her close.

Kyrie wasn't even concerned with her presence potentially hindering females from trying him. He had one or two females that he rocked with when he got horny, and they didn't play the club like that. In fact, one of them went to church every

Wednesday and every Sunday. She played that good girl role to a *T*, but she was one of the biggest freaks that he'd ever met.

"Thank you for inviting me," Khelani replied showing off stark white teeth.

"You can roll with me. I have the entire VIP section on lock."

"Damn who is this?" Tae inquired as he looked Khelani up and down.

When Kyrie answered, he shot Tae a look that only he could read. He was silently telling him that Khelani was off limits. "This is Khelani. She's my new administrative assistant. Khelani, this is my homie Tae."

"Nice to meet you."

The small group headed inside the club and was immediately ushered into the VIP section. The club was packed and when they entered the section, Kobie, and around thirty more people were already lit. Thick weed smoke lingered in the air, and the bottles of liquor seemed to be never ending.

"What up boss man?" Kobie greeted Kyrie with a home boy hug.

Kyrie introduced Kobie to Khelani, then he passed him the black box that he brought inside the club.

"Happy birthday my nigga. May this year be even greater than the last."

Kobie opened the box and lost his cool when he saw the diamond encrusted chain. "This shit is sick," he screamed and bounced around the club section showing it off.

Kobie was a good kid. He was twenty, and he signed his deal at the age of eighteen. With his advance money, he bought his mom a house, and he bought his dream car. After that, he worked hard, and the fame came fast. He had a whole slew of cousins and friends that felt entitled to his money and finally after spending thousands upon thousands of dollars loaning people money that they never paid back, paying the bills of a good 5 people every month, bailing niggas out of jail, etc. he got fed up and cut a lot of people off. He had purchased jewelry for himself, but the $19,000 necklace that Kyrie gifted him was the most expensive gift he'd ever received in his life. Shit, aside from Kyrie and the other artists at the label, nobody else even got Kobie a birthday gift except his mom and his girl. He damn near cried when his girlfriend gifted him ten pairs of sneakers. It was the thoughtfulness. Everyone else assumed that because he was rich that he didn't need other people to buy him gifts, but Kobie just wanted to know he was appreciated. The gift didn't even have to be expensive.

"You give good gifts," Khelani stated as a bottle girl came by and handed Kyrie a bottle of Hennessey.

"Thank you. He works hard. He deserves it." He eyed a stack of cups on the table. "Would you like a drink?"

"Umm sure, but I already drank some Don Julio. I can't do that dark."

"No problem. I see some right over there. I'll be right back."

Khelani watched him walk over to retrieve the bottle. Kyrie was handsome indeed. She killed Malachi a month before she left North Carolina, so it had only been two months since she'd been with a man. She wasn't pressed, and she stayed too busy to be lonely, but she wondered for a brief moment what it would be like to wet his beard up. Shit, she was still human, and she still got urges. If she was going to let him get her rocks off, she knew she'd need to do it before he found out who she was. Sometimes, all women wanted was the dick too. Kemp had been on her ass since she was a preteen, so Khelani had never been in love. Not even once. She came close to it at seventeen but when Kemp found out, he deaded that shit. Khelani didn't lose her virginity until she was twenty. In her entire life, she'd been with two men.

"Thank you," she took the drink that Kyrie handed to her.

"Would it be awkward if I asked you out? I'm not even gon' stand here and pretend like I'm not intrigued by you. You working for me makes me a bit hesitant to cross the lines, but I see you as being mature enough to handle it. No pressure. Just two grown single people hanging out off the clock. What do you say?"

He was cute enough for her to fantasize about, but Khelani hadn't really expected him to ask her out. Even if there would be no love connection, in an effort to keep him close, she agreed.

"What do you have in mind?"

"Maybe dinner tomorrow evening. I can get my homie to close up his restaurant and cook us a gang of good shit. His food is the truth, and I'm a silent partner."

"Impressive. Sure, we can do that."

"Bet. I'm going to go mingle a lil' bit instead of staying stuck up under you like a sucka. Watch out for these niggas 'cus they gon' be on you. Better yet, maybe I should stay."

Khelani laughed. "I'll be fine. I see Kim over there."

Kyrie did a double take as he saw Camila and Anya entering the section.

"Yo, that chick right there do you know her? The two of you could pass for sisters."

"We are sisters."

"Damn. At least I know I'm not tripping. Well, now I feel better about walking off. I'll text you a time for our date."

"Got it," Khelani smiled.

"Okay, I see you with the fine man all in ya face," Anya joked as she hugged her sister while Camila smirked.

Anya's sister was just as gorgeous as her, and she looked like Kyrie's type. Especially if she was the stick in the mud that Anya had described. Kyrie didn't like lit bitches. He liked boring women, and he still didn't even wife them, so Camila knew all he wanted to do was stick dick to this chick.

Anya made introductions and right away, Khelani got bad vibes. "This is my sissy Khelani, and this is my boss and friend, and Kyrie's cousin, Camila."

"Nice to meet you," Khelani gave her a fake smile. Camila was dressed in a black dress that was completely see through. Her nipples were on full display. She didn't even try to put on pasties or anything. Khelani could see right away why Anya gravitated to her because that was for sure some shit she'd wear.

The women chatted for a few and when Kyrie came over, Khelani could damn near feel the heat radiating off of him.

"Girl, what the fuck you got on?" he spat in a tone full of disdain. "Aye, I'm 'bout to walk the fuck away from you 'cus you tripping like a muhfucka. Have some respect for yourself."

Camila rolled her eyes upwards.

"Here you go being all extra and shit. They're just breasts damn. I can't help it I'm not one of those boring ass church hoes that you like to fuck."

Kyrie didn't even respond. He simply walked off. Khelani peeped the slight shade. She wasn't dumb. She didn't like Camila's ass off rip but unless she came right out and disrespected her, she'd spare the little thot. Khelani wanted to stay far away from her, and she hoped that Anya didn't find her way into trouble with this hoe. Just as Khelani finished off her drink, her phone rang. When she looked down and saw that Kasim was calling her, she walked off. There wasn't a place in the club that she could go where music wouldn't be loud, but she didn't want to talk to him in front of Anya or a stranger. Anya was no longer apart of family business. Khelani walked towards the bathroom and stuck one finger in her ear to block some of the noise.

"Hello?"

"Just hitting you to let you know that I'm about to go meet James. I told him I don't do this late night shit, but he just got back in town. I'm making an exception because he's spending double what he spent last time."

Khelani's eyebrows furrowed. Delante wasn't in town yet, and she didn't like the thought of Kasim going to make a play at damn near one in the morning alone.

"Swing by the club and get me. I don't want you going alone."

"Khelani no. Don't insult me. I'm a grown ass man. I can conduct business without you being with me."

Khelani rolled her eyes upwards and kissed her teeth. "It doesn't matter what my gender is. I'm an extra set of eyes, and we don't know this nigga to trust him. I'm going with you. I'll text you the address, and you just call me when you're outside." She ended the call before he could protest.

"Oh, my bad," Khelani stated when she turned around and ran into Kyrie.

"Nah it's my bad for not paying attention. That damn Camila has me hot," he shook his head.

Anya chuckled. "If she's anything like my sister, she keeps you hot then. I learned long ago to stop even caring. Let her figure life out on her own. She's grown."

"I feel you, but the shit she be doing isn't even called for. You good though?"

"Yeah. Something actually came up, and I have to leave in a few."

Kyrie eyed her intensely. What could come up this time of night but sex? Maybe a nigga hit her and told her he was about to come scoop her. She told him she was single, but that didn't mean she wasn't fucking someone. He peered into her eyes and envisioned what it would be like to slide up in her. Was another nigga about to do that?

65

"We still on for tomorrow?"

"Yes. Of course."

"Aight. Be safe, and I'll text you."

Khelani smiled and walked away while Kyrie shook his head to himself. He was putting too much thought into where she might be going. Technically, it wasn't his business. He wasn't even on that kind of time to be caring what a female did, but he was learning fast that Khelani wasn't too much like most women, and that shit had him curious as hell.

"DAMN, YOU FUCKED UP," Snow bit his bottom lip and narrowed his eyes at Anya who was sitting on the couch in his friend's den. He damn sure couldn't take her to his mama's house, and he didn't want to get a room when he wasn't sure if they would link. He kept thinking she was bullshitting but in actuality, she was trying to get away from Camila.

Snow stayed with his mom or different homeboys whenever him and Caresha were on the outs. If he fucked Anya and the pussy was good, he'd have no problem splurging on hotel rooms to fuck her thick ass in. Caresha had a pretty face, and he loved her to death, but not even birthing three kids gave her an ass. He always joked that he was going to buy her one, but they broke up so much, he was scared to. He would be damned if he paid for her to get her body done and she went and fucked the next man. He'd kill her ass for real.

"I feel good as shit. Why you all the way over there?" she purred. Her lids were so low from weed and liquor that it looked like her eyes were closed.

"You want me over there with you?" Snow licked his lips. He walked over to Anya with his hand on his semi-hard dick.

"Let me see that shit," she giggled moving his hand out of

the way and reaching inside to feel what he was working with. There was nothing shy about Anya.

She didn't have as much luck at the party as she had anticipated, but she was so drunk and high that at the moment, she didn't care. A famous producer asked for her number, but there was no guarantee that he'd call. A rapper wanted to take her home, but he wanted her to have a threesome with another bitch from the club, and she wasn't with that. Maybe if she already had him locked in, and she did it with him on some wild fun shit. But she wasn't about to compete with another bitch the very first time that she had sex with a nigga. Anya knew she was a freak, and her pussy was good for sure but if he couldn't be satisfied with just her, fuck him.

"Ummmm," she moaned when she saw he was working with a nice size. It was thick and long. Not huge, but she could definitely work with the shit.

"You like that shit?" he asked in a low tone.

Anya didn't answer. She just pulled it out and studied it for a bit. She had no interest in playing the good girl role. She didn't have to wait until the fifth or sixth time to give him head. Anya enjoyed giving head. She liked seeing the faces men made and the whimpers and moans that her fellatio caused. The ultimate foreplay for her, was making a nigga putty in her hands. Anya took Snow's dick into her mouth, and he let out a low guttural moan as the head of his wood touched the back of her throat. Anya slowly pulled back then laced his shaft with spit. She rotated her wrist and slowly began to jack him off while she sucked him. Anya's eyelids fluttered as she went in on his dick and seconds later, Snow was moaning and fucking her face. Anya's dick sucking skills had his toes curling and his breathing shallow.

Anya pulled her head back, smirked and wiped her mouth as she stood up to undress. Her pussy was wet from sucking

Snow off, and now she wanted to be pounded. Snow followed her lead and undressed as well. After securing a condom onto his dick, he grabbed Anya's C cup breasts and ran his tongue back and forth across her large nipples. Ready to get the party started, Anya slipped a finger between her moist folds and rubbed her clit while he sucked. She had the engine humming so by the time he twirled her around and bent her over the couch, slid his dick in her and hit her with a few strokes, Anya was screaming bloody murder while she came all on his dick.

Remembering that he was a guest in someone else's home, Snow clasped a hand around Anya's mouth to silence her cries of pleasure while he continued to drill into her. His balls slapped against her pussy as he fucked her savagely with one hand around her mouth. When she quieted her cries, he moved his hand down to her neck and began to choke her, and that instantly made Anya have another orgasm.

"Got damn," Snow panted as Anya creamed on his dick a second time. He was fascinated by the sight of her fat ass and loving how wet and juicy her honeypot was.

Anya reached behind her and spread her ass cheeks wide. "Got damn you got some fire ass pussy," Snow gritted as he tried to hold back from cumming so fast.

Anya let go of the back of the couch and leaned down and grabbed her ankles. Snow hissed as he slowed his strokes and watched his dick slide in and out of Anya's tight pink flower. His body jerked slightly, and that's when he knew she had him. He was hooked on Anya's pussy already. Once he quickened the pace of his strokes, it didn't take long for his seeds to shoot from his dick and into the condom. He wished he could have spent the entire night in her pussy, but it wasn't his crib. Snow slid out of Anya and smacked her ass.

"We def got to get a hotel room next time. Or do you think your sister would trip if you had company?"

"Boy I'm grown," Anya rolled her eyes. Khelani couldn't tell her not to have company, but Anya did want freedom. She didn't want to have to pay bills, but she wanted to be able to do what she wanted without Khelani breathing down her neck.

"Plus, I'm getting my own spot soon."

Snow's eyes lit up at the sound of that. He made good money customizing grills, but he also sold a little coke on the side, so he wasn't broke by far. The idea of Anya having her own crib that he could fuck her in for hours had him ready to trick.

"Let me know when you find a place. I'll def put something on that deposit for you."

Anya only smirked. Shit, he needed to have the whole thing. What the fuck was something? She told herself to just be patient and she'd find the baller that she needed to come and be her savior. Anya was lowkey irritated that she had to take an Uber home rather than just curling up and going to sleep. She gave Snow a pass this time. The sex was good, and she'd keep him around. For now. But it was clear to her that Snow wouldn't be that nigga that came in and tricked on her heavy. At this rate, Anya needed about two more niggas to add to her team. One thing was for sure. She wouldn't be missing another night of work anytime soon.

Chapter Seven

"This is a cliché ass question, but why are you single? It's got to be by choice," Kyrie inquired the next day over dinner. He wanted to pick Khelani up, but she had insisted on meeting him at the Brazilian Steakhouse.

She showed up dressed in a tight black dress, red peep toe booties, and her hair was back curly. Three gold chains with different charms graced her neck and on her wrist, was an iced out Cartier watch. She matched his fly for real, and Kyrie wanted to know her story.

"My father has always had high expectations of me. There was no room for boys when he wanted me to get straight A's and every time I met one goal, there was another for me to cross off the list. I just never slowed down enough to get into anything serious. The few times I attempted, my trust was broken, and I quickly found out that there was a motive or lies involved. I don't have time for that. I'd rather get to the money than have a man playing me and stressing me out."

"I can relate for sure, but it seems weird to hear a woman

say that. It's really niggas out here fucking over beautiful ass smart women that get her own money? That's crazy."

Khelani chuckled. "Yes there are really men out here doing that, but I'm good. I'd rather be the way I am than stuck in some relationship I hate or bouncing from man to man because I don't know how to, or I don't want to take care of myself. A man can provide me dick and companionship. That's about it because I take care of myself. Oddly, that's what most men have problems with. They have no problem throwing money and fucking but ask them to be honest or emotionally available and it's crickets."

"Damn." That was really all Kyrie could say because she had described him. He was emotionally unavailable like a muhfucka. He damn near loved the fact that women would fuck him with no conversation based off just who he was. It was rare that Kyrie had to work for the pussy. All this getting to know a person and going out on dates, he was doing it with Khelani because he wanted to. "So, you're good not being in a relationship?" He knew some females that were too into running the streets and hoeing to settle down, but he knew most women really wanted white picket fences and babies.

Khelani thought about how stupid she felt when she let her guard down for Malachi, and he attempted to rob her. She couldn't afford another slip up like that, and she wasn't trying to go to prison for murder. She needed to stay far away from niggas that made her want to pump their asses full of lead.

"For the moment, yes. Maybe in a few years, I'll have a change of heart."

Kyrie studied Khelani to see if she was just kicking game. Something was telling him that her cool ass wasn't playing a part. She didn't seem like the type to be too pressed about a nigga, and that lowkey excited Kyrie. He wanted to be the exception to the rule. The one that made her fold.

"I hear that. What do you do for fun?"

"I like to read."

That got a laugh out of Kyrie. "I said fun Khelani."

She raised her eyebrows and tried to figure out what was funny. "I know what you said, and I read for fun. When I have time."

"My bad," he continued to laugh. "You talk a lot about being busy. You just started at the record company, and you get off at five. You got other jobs I don't know about?"

Khelani smirked. "Maybe. Now, let's talk about you. Why are you single?"

Kyrie cut into his steak. "It's just hard to find a woman that's 'bout something." He thought for a second. "Okay, I'm lying. What I said is true, but I have trust issues as well. I like a different kind of female. One that is smart, classy, gets her own money without fucking for it, and not out here trying to be a hot girl. I have found some women over the years that fit that criteria, but I have trust issues. I don't trust easily at all, and it's hard to be in a relationship if you don't trust your partner."

"I feel you one hundred percent. I feel like if some shit is meant to be, then that's what it will be."

"Fa' sho'. Listen, I'll be flying out to Cali next week for the BET awards. You want to come?"

"What about work?"

"I'm flying out on a Thursday and coming back Sunday. You'll only miss two days in the office, but it's cool. It's a work trip. You can bring a laptop and work on my private jet. You can also work at the hotel."

Delante had come into town, so Kasim had help. Khelani wouldn't feel so bad about leaving him while she went to Cali. Unlike Anya, she didn't want to put everything on Kasim. It took a team to run an empire, but this trip could help her in the long run. Plus, she'd been working hard as hell for two years. She deserved a small break.

"Sure. I can go."

A grin graced Kyrie's face. "Cool. I'll book your room when I get back home. I know you're against relationships and all, but maybe we can hang out a bit in Cali. Have some fun off the clock."

"You're not worried about rumors or what people may say?"

"Hell nah. I'm the boss. I run this shit, and I do what I want."

"I heard that," Khelani replied before finishing off her wine.

Their plates were both clean, and Kyrie damn near hated to go. "Dinner has truly been nice Ms. Khelani. I enjoyed your company."

"Likewise."

After he paid the bill and left a tip, he walked Khelani out to her car. Kyrie was itching to taste her lips, palm her ass, suck her breasts, or something. He was going to play it cool, however. As if the Universe knew he was done eating, his phone rang as he was walking back to his car. "Yo?" he greeted Tae.

"We lost another one. Derrick not reing up with us this time either."

Kyrie pinched the bridge of his nose and closed his eyes. When he spoke, his tone was low and even. "Find out who in the fuck is selling weed to all my got damn customers." He ended the call without even waiting for Tae respond. When Kyrie found out who this muhfucka was, he might just toss her ass in a river with bricks tied to her feet.

"You TRYING to come back to the room with me or what?" Mozzy spoke into Anya's ear as he hugged her from behind while she danced on his lap. His dick was harder than Chinese arithmetic, and he'd already tipped her ass $200. He was tired of flirting. He wanted to fuck.

Men had been buying Anya drinks all night, and she was feeling good. Being the new girl in the club got her a lot of attention, and it was all welcomed. She had been at the club for four hours and had earned $945. There were two more hours before closing, so she knew she'd be leaving with over $1,000.

"I still have two more hours to dance. I need my money," she replied as she stood up because the song had ended.

Mozzy eyed her thick thighs, and he was ready to trick heavy on Anya's sexy ass. He had just started making money with Kyrie, but it was good ass money. Kyrie told him that his suite was paid up for another two weeks. It was nothing to him because he used a business credit card, and he would write the room off on his taxes but once the money started coming in, Mozzy would have to foot his own bill. Mozzy was still enjoying the free ride for the moment, and he was feeling good.

"How much will it take for you to leave with me right now?"

Anya smirked. She wasn't sure what Mozzy was working with, and she knew if she said too high a number, he may not be able to swing it. However, she wasn't going to completely lowball herself. He'd already given her $200, so she decided to cut him a little slack. "If I leave here now, I'll be missing out on no less than $500."

That wasn't what Mozzy wanted to hear. He only had $1,000 in his pocket after splurging at the mall earlier but fuck it. You only live once. A group of niggas walking by openly admired Anya's ass, and that was the deciding factor for him. The cognac in his system had him feeling like a real boss nigga.

The money he spent on Anya, he'd make it right back. That was the point of fast money, right? If you couldn't have fun with it, why risk your freedom and your life to make it?

"Bet. Let's roll."

"Slow down daddy. I have to cash out and get dressed. Give me fifteen minutes."

Of what she'd earned, she owed Camila $141. Strippers had to give her 15% of their money at the end of the night. Anya was glad that Mozzy was giving her the $500 off the record, and that she didn't have to give Camila a portion of that. Anya knocked on the door and walked into the office before Camila even said come in. When she stepped in the office, Camila pushed her desk drawer shut. "Damn, did you hear me say come in?"

Anya could have sworn she saw a white powdery substance on the tip of Camila's nose, but she swiped her hand over her face fast as hell so if it had been there, she swept it away before Anya could be for sure. Maybe she was tripping. Anya frowned her face up slightly, because it wasn't like Camila to be a sour puss. She was normally bubbly and lit.

"My bad. Geesh, I was just coming to cash out. I'm about to head out."

Camila's eyes narrowed. "Why you leaving so early? There's money out there." She wasn't stupid. If a stripper was leaving the club while money was flowing, they were more than likely going to fuck, and that cut into Camila's money. Still, there was only so much she could say because the strippers were grown, and they didn't punch a clock. They could dance two hours or six hours.

"I'm about to go kick it with Mozzy for a bit."

Camila didn't even attempt to hide her disgust. "Mozzy? Ewww. He ain't got no money. That nigga is Kyrie's errand boy. You 'bout to miss out on scrilla for that lame nigga?"

Anya didn't give a damn about Mozzy. She didn't care what Camila said about him technically, but she didn't like the way Camila was looking at her. She acted like Anya was about to go fuck a bum on the street. Shit in all, she was getting $700 out of Mozzy in one night. He wasn't that damn broke.

"You act like you in that nigga's pockets. Him running Kyrie's errands don't concern me. Every night he comes in here, he tips me lovely. I'm just going to have some fun. Damn."

"I thought you were about your bread. Leaving the club two hours early to entertain a broke nigga isn't bad bitch behavior, but do you boo."

Anya was feisty by nature, but it intensified when she had alcohol in her system. "Who the fuck are you to be judging me? I don't have to sit in this bitch all night if I don't want. First, I couldn't fuck with Snow. Now, you're telling me don't fuck with Mozzy. I wasn't aware you were the pussy police."

Camila eyed Anya with a sadistic smirk before she responded. "Slow ya muhfuckin' roll shawty. I don't run you or your pussy, but I run this shit. Hell nah, you can't fuck with Snow. That's my homegirl's nigga, and I'd be a wack bitch to let you deal with him. As far as Mozzy, if you want to give your pussy up to broke niggas and bring down your stock, that's on you. Now you can get the fuck out of my office."

Anya was stunned. Her and Camila had hit it off instantly from day one and now, they were getting disrespectful with one another. Anya could tell by Camila's dilated pupils that she probably had seen white powder on her nose. Anya was all about partying and having fun, but not even she fucked with coke. Deciding to leave before shit got ugly, Anya got up out of Camila's office. At the end of the day, her father was rich, and her sister had big bank. She'd rather go crawling back to Khelani and work for their father before she kissed Camila's ass. Matter of fact, that's what she'd do. With a smirk on her face, she headed for the dressing room. Her first order of business would be to try and secure Snow as a customer for her sister. Khelani only sold weight, but Snow smoked mad weed. Anya was sure that once he tried Khelani's shit that he'd at least cop an ounce. True weed smokers didn't cop a couple of grams a day. Not the ones with money. They'd go ahead and buy enough weed to last them a couple days. Maybe even a couple of weeks.

Yeah, fuck that raggedy ass strip club. And even if she did want to keep dancing, there were plenty of strip clubs in the A, and Camila's wasn't the most popping by far. Fucking bitch.

Chapter Eight

"You're going to the BET awards? Man, what the fuck? I want to goooo," Anya whined like a damn kid.

Khelani shook her head at her sister's slight temper tantrum. "It's not my trip. Kyrie is the one with the private jet and the tickets to the show. Sorry."

"You could have given me a heads up or something. Fuck." Anya was pissed. How was she in a city full of rich niggas, and she hadn't snagged one yet? She damn near wished she hadn't gotten into it with Camila about Mozzy's ass. Whether he gave her money or not, he was the worst lay she ever had in her life. She was never sleeping with him again.

"I'm sure you'll be okay."

"Anyway," Anya let out a dramatic sigh. "I smoked a blunt with my homie this morning, and he wants to cop two ounces of weed from you. Since you're going out of town, you want me to get Kasim to serve him?"

Khelani couldn't believe that Anya rounded up some clientele for her. She almost told her to serve him, but she wasn't going to give Anya the code to the safe that her weed was stashed in. Nah. She hadn't proven herself to be worthy of all that.

"Thank you. Yeah. Hit Kasim. I have to get ready to go."

"Uggghhhhhhh," Anya groaned loudly, and Khelani only laughed.

When she applied to work at the record company, there were a few vacant positions. When Khelani suggested she apply too, Anya looked at her like she had two heads. Anya didn't want to go out and work for shit. She wanted everything just given to her based off her looks, her body, or her name, and life didn't always work like that. Khelani's Uber arrived, and she headed downstairs. It was in the back of her mind that Kyrie probably didn't invite her on the trip just for business purposes. Khelani knew that any fun she planned on having with him would have to be short-lived. When her six weeks at the label were up and she quit, she wouldn't be seeing him again. She wasn't even sure how she was going to explain leaving the label so soon after starting, but she'd think of something. Time was moving fast. She'd already been there for two weeks. Khelani only had four weeks left to do what she needed to do.

She had to leave the party early to go be with Kasim, so maybe this trip to the awards would make up for that. Quite a few of the artists and employees of the label would be on the jet. Khelani didn't want to just jump into business. She wanted to develop a nice cordial relationship first then ease in the fact that she sold weed. A lot of rappers popped various kinds of pills, drank lean, and some even snorted coke, but it seemed like all them smoked weed. There was always money to be made in the marijuana business, and people with money loved paying top dollar for shit. It made them feel like they were purchasing something exclusive that the average person couldn't afford. Khelani knew how to take advantage of that.

Khelani had only been in the car for five minutes, and she had ten new emails. Her job wasn't hard, but it wasn't exactly laid back. She worked every hour that she was on the clock. There was never a moment to waste unless she wanted to get backed up. Khelani was so focused on replying to emails and trying to get caught up on her work load that she didn't even realize they had pulled up to the location the jet was leaving from until the driver opened the door for her.

"Oh wow, I was in a zone for real. Thank you."

"You're welcome."

The driver collected her luggage, and she followed him over to the jet. Kyrie had pulled up in a black Hummer, and he exited the vehicle dressed in black sweats, a black hoodie, and black sneakers. The ice around his neck and encrusted in his watch seemed to shine brighter against his all black attire. His beard glistened in the sun, and Khelani could tell he'd moisturized it. There was nothing like a man that took care of himself. The fact that he smiled when he saw her might have made Khelani blush, if she was into that kind of thing. The last nigga that made her blush had tried to rob her, so she was good on that emotional shit.

"What up?" he shocked Khelani by giving her a one arm hug. "How was the ride here?"

"It was cool. The driver was very polite."

"That's what's up. I need to run something by you."

Khelani looked at him curiously. "What's that?"

Kyrie looked a little hesitant to respond. He swiped his hand across the back of his neck. "So, one of the chicks that be styling my artist, Swag, she's coming out tomorrow. She has her own room, and we're not together. But we've slept together more than a few times and when she sees other women around, she tries to be on that territorial shit. She'll probably be doing little shit to make it seem like we're together, but we're not. I never lied to you. I'm single."

Khelani shrugged passively. "That's fine. You don't owe me any explanations. We're two people that had dinner together once. I am not tripping. Trust."

Kyrie nodded. "I just wanted to make sure."

Khelani followed him onto the jet, and she spoke to everyone that was already onboard. Kyrie for sure seemed like the type of man to have sex with lots of different women. Khelani had never fucked him, and she was still on the fence as to if she would. She didn't care about one of his women being on the trip as long as the bitch didn't get disrespectful. She sat across from Kim, and the women alternated between conversing and working the entire trip.

"Yo, your eyes are pretty as hell. I know you be having niggas mesmerized and shit," one of the rappers assigned to the label, Draco, said to Khelani randomly. She was used to it. People had been admiring her eyes her entire life.

When she looked up from her laptop, she saw Kyrie looking in her direction. She turned towards Draco. "Thank you, but I don't know about all that," she chuckled.

Draco licked his lips. "You single ma?"

Khelani had to stifle her laughter. Draco wasn't more than nineteen. Because he was famous and had money, he was probably used to pulling any woman he wanted regardless of his age, but Khelani wasn't with it. He was cute but rich or not, she couldn't do a damn thing with a nigga that couldn't even buy her a drink legally in a bar. Rather than wounding his ego or hurting his pride, she just smiled at him politely.

"I am, but I don't mix business with pleasure. You cute though."

She was glad that Draco's phone rang, because he looked as

if he was about to protest what she'd just said. The jet finally landed in LA, and Khelani was eager to get off and stretch her legs. There were eleven of them total, so they split up into three SUV's at the landing strip. Khelani ended up in the same vehicle as Kyrie.

"You trying to join me for dinner tonight?"

She looked over at him curiously. "Isn't your lil' boo coming tomorrow?" Khelani knew good and well he wasn't going to try and squeeze her in for a quick fuck and then be all up on the other chick when she came.

"I explained the reason to you why I even brought that shit up. Don't hold that against me. I haven't had sex with Rebecca in a minute, and I don't plan on it because she does too much. She's a good stylist though, and Swag doesn't want anybody styling him but her, so I tolerate her. I don't fuck with her like that anymore but if she sees a beautiful woman around, she will try to make it seem like we're still rocking. I've checked her about the shit, and she still acts dumb."

Khelani didn't want him to keep explaining because it really didn't matter. She didn't care what Kyrie did or who he did it with. "We'll see. If I'm not tired."

Kyrie raised one eyebrow as if he felt like she was bullshitting. He couldn't force her to fuck with him. He was trying to go with the flow and let things unfold naturally, but he wanted to rock with her for certain. He was pissed when Swag requested that Rebecca come on the trip, but he had to put business above all else. He knew Rebecca though and as soon as she saw Khelani, she would start doing the most. He was dreading the shit. She wasn't the type to disrespect Khelani or try to fight her. She'd just be extra with the affection towards Kyrie.

"You do that," was all he said.

Khelani had spoke about not being interested in a relationship, and he wasn't really either. But he'd be lying if he said he wasn't attracted to Khelani or if he said he didn't want to see how things would play out with them.

———————————

ANYA WALKED out of the bathroom with a towel wrapped around her thick body and steam from the bathroom wafting down the hallway behind her. When the song she was listening to stopped playing, she knew that someone was about to call her. She was shocked to see that Camila was calling her phone. For a brief moment, she started not to answer, but she went ahead and picked up.

"Hello?"

"You coming to work tonight?" Camila asked in a pleasant tone as if they hadn't just gotten into it the night before.

Anya wasn't sure how to answer. Should she just say she was quitting because she didn't want to work for a bitch? She quickly decided that she wasn't about to let Camila or anyone else punk her into not being truthful. "I really hadn't planned on coming back, since it seemed that we aren't on the same page."

Camila kissed her teeth. "Anya my business consists of baby-sitting hella bitches that half the time don't do what they should be doing. I run an entire club alone plus have to keep my eye on everything and everyone and sometimes, I just get stressed the fuck out. It's not okay for me to get frustrated and take my anger out on anyone that works for me. It's not professional, and I'm working on my attitude. I value your presence in my club and if you come in tonight, you won't even have to cash out. Don't tell those other bitches though."

Anya smiled to herself as she grabbed her bottle of lotion

and sat on the bed. She liked how Camila was humbling herself. "Well, since you put it like that, I'll be there for sure."

"Great!"

Anya really wasn't feeling how Camila could switch up at the drop of a dime, but as long as she didn't have to cash out at the end of the night, she'd be there. She could already see how nasty Camila could be when she was angry, and she didn't like it. No matter how sincere her apology seemed, her coming at Anya wrong could happen again. Her father always told her that people show you the real them when they're angry. Camila was trying to appease Anya, but Anya was smart enough to know that Camila still had that boss bitch mentality and in the midst of an argument, she wouldn't hesitate to let it be known that she felt Anya was beneath her.

Anya chuckled to herself. "Bitch has no idea who my father or even my sister is. Couple of Chanel bags and a hole in the wall club don't make you better than the next. Her net worth probably looks like lunch money compared to Khelani."

After standing up and letting the towel drop to the floor, Anya admired her naked frame in the mirror. She was too damn bad not to be on the arm of a rich nigga. She should have been on a jet on her way to the BET awards. She honestly could have been even without a nigga if her father would just act right. Anya hated that he was so damn difficult. Why couldn't she just be a spoiled Trinidadian princess? As Anya was stepping into a red thong, her phone rang again. She kissed her teeth when she saw that Mozzy was calling. This was his third time calling her since they had sex, and she hadn't answered any of his calls. She wished he would just get the hint already.

Her first issue with him was that his dick was too fucking small. The only way it wouldn't slip out of her every five minutes was if he put her legs all the way up until they were damn near behind her head. Her ass had to basically be lifted off the bed while she was damn near on her head in order for his tiny penis to stay inside of her. Anya was all for different positions but having to stay that way for too long was uncomfortable. His sex game was just garbage. She even hated kissing him. The traces of salvia he left on her skin after kissing on her, disgusted Anya. She loved money with a passion, but he couldn't pay her any amount of money for her to have sex with him again. If she got broke enough, she'd slang pounds with Khelani before she fucked him again.

Once her phone stopped ringing, Anya finished getting dressed and headed to the club. Since she hadn't planned on going, Anya arrived at the club later than she normally would, and it was already kind of packed. She rushed to the dressing room to undress. She wasn't trying to miss out on too much more money. When she came back out, she had fifteen minutes before she had to do her set on stage, so she sauntered through the crowd trying to find good prospects to flirt with. Anya stopped dead in her tracks when she noticed Mozzy leaning against the bar eye fucking her. As soon as they locked eyes, she turned in the opposite direction to go to the bar on the other side of the club. The sight of him turned her fucking stomach. Why wasn't his ass in California with Kyrie? Camila was right. He wasn't shit but an errand boy, and the thrill with kicking it with him was gone. Anya just hated that he could pop up on her at anytime when she was at work. It really didn't matter though because like Camila, she could be a nasty bitch when she needed to be. If she had to hurt Mozzy's feelings in order for him to get the point, then she would.

Mozzy's eyes narrowed as he watched Khelani's plump ass walk away from him. The cognac he was sipping burned his throat, but that was no match for the boiling that his blood was doing. He didn't have an issue fucking a chick once and then cutting her ass off, unless he'd spent a lot of money on her. Him giving Anya $700 in one night was more than he'd ever given any female at one time. Now, this bitch was trying to play him? Fair exchange wasn't robbery but in Mozzy's eyes, there was no fair exchange. For as much money as he'd given that bitch, he needed to be able to get some of that pussy a few more times. It was the best that Mozzy had since he'd been home from prison, and he didn't appreciate being curved. Anya was the type of chick that he could wife. It didn't matter that she was a stripper. Once he started making real money with Kyrie, he could spoil her, and she could quit the club.

His nostrils flared as he saw a nigga with blonde dreads grab Anya by the wrist. She stopped to talk to him and even from across the room, Mozzy could see the wide smile on her face. That was his bad for falling for a hoe. It was a lesson that he was learning the hard way but if it was up to him, he wouldn't be the only one learning a lesson. If Anya thought she was just going to ghost him, that bitch was 'bout to find out just how Mozzy from Houston got down.

Chapter Nine

Khelani was standing at the bathroom sink with a towel wrapped around her body moisturizing her wet curls. She had taken a shower and was going to get dressed to go out with Kim and a few other employees of the label. There were parties going on everywhere. She was finally getting a mini vacation from running around selling weed and sitting behind a desk for eight hours a day, and she was going to enjoy it. There was a knock on her room door, and Khelani's eyebrows snapped together. Who would be at her door? Maybe it was Kim. Khelani pulled the towel off her body and grabbed a white oversized shirt. After pulling it over her head, she stuck her feet in some slippers and walked to the door. Khelani didn't care how nice the hotel was. She wasn't walking barefoot on a carpet that strange people trekked on with their shoes on.

She raised one eyebrow after looking out of the peephole and seeing that Kyrie was standing at the door. After slowly pulling the door open, both her eyebrows hiked up. "May I help you?"

"Yeah. I'm here to pick you up for our dinner date."

"Ummmm," Khelani scratched her head. "I don't remember agreeing to go out on a date with you. Plus, you didn't give me a time and as you can see, I'm not even dressed."

"I'll wait," he stated and walked into the room leaving her looking confused.

After standing there for a few seconds stuck on stupid, she closed the door. "Why do you assume that I don't have plans? You do know that Kim asked me to go out with her, Bella, and Maria."

"They can wait. It won't take us more than two hours to grab dinner. Damn, you act like I'm the worst person in the world to hang out with."

Khelani chuckled. "I never said that. Don't put words in my mouth."

"So, I'll wait for you to get dressed, and we can roll." Kyrie sat down on the couch in the front of her suite, and Khelani let out a deep breath. He obviously wasn't taking no for an answer, so she headed back into the bathroom.

After moisturizing her face and skin, she grabbed an outfit from her suitcase, went back in the bathroom, and closed the door. Once she was dressed, Khelani emerged from the bathroom with light make up on her face. Kyrie watched her in awe as she reached for her shoes. She had on a red see through type dress that was similar to the one that Camila wore with all her breasts exposed, but Khelani wore hers in a classy way. She wore a black bra underneath and even though it was a dress technically and came down to her ankles, she wore black skinny jeans underneath. On her feet, she put nude strappy heels. Nude lipstick coated her lips, and eyeliner accentuated her almond shaped eyes.

Hanging from her ears were large gold hoops, and a matching gold watch decorated her wrist. Khelani looked like pure fuckin' perfection. Camila could take some tips from her on how to be sexy while having respect for herself. Kyrie thought to himself.

"You look fuckin' phenomenal," Kyrie admired as she grabbed her purse.

Khelani turned around with a smirk. "I don't look like a boring church lady, do I? I heard that's the kind of woman you like."

Kyrie frowned. "Camila thinks any woman that doesn't show everything God gave her is boring. I wouldn't listen to her hating ass. I like women that have respect for themselves and carry themselves like a grown ass woman. That's what I like."

"Nothing wrong with that. I told you your cousin reminds me a lot of my sister. There is no reasoning with them or trying to get them to think normal most times."

"Tell me about it. You ready to go?"

"Yeah. Mind telling me where we're going?"

Kyrie held the door open for her. "I always have to hit The Melting Pot when I come to LA. The food is amazing."

Khelani's eyes swept over Kyrie while they were in the elevator, and she had to admit that he was handsome as fuck. She could see why a woman with little self-restraint and low self-esteem may do the most in an effort to keep other women away from him. That would never be her thing, but Khelani knew everyone wasn't as strong as her. She couldn't imagine the heartbreak that weaker willed women went through. For as tough as she tried to be, Malachi came along and made her feel things she'd never felt before. As soon as she went against the grain and let him in, he did the unthinkable. Killing him hurt her, but it also further numbed her.

Khelani would be damned if she made the same mistake twice. It didn't matter how sexy, rich, or charming Kyrie was. Their time getting to know one another would be coming to an end soon. She was going to make sure of that. The only way she'd keep contact with him any longer would be if he decided to get his weed from her, and she doubted his pride would allow him to do so.

Kyrie led her out to a black Escalade where a driver was waiting for him. He wanted to rent a Porsche, or something fly as fuck for his short stay in LA, but he figured there was no need. He planned to turn up and have fun, so with all the champagne and liquor that would be flowing, having his own personal driver was best. Kyrie also knew that if he was riding around LA with Khelani, that paparazzi was sure to see them and take pictures. He didn't even know where shit with her was going to go, so he didn't want extra eyes and ears in his business. Inside the car, Kyrie's phone was going off nonstop, but he gave Khelani his undivided attention. There was still a lot that he didn't know about her and there was a lot of mystery that left him intrigued, but he didn't need to be intrigued. He needed to know who she was. Kyrie got his people in HR to run a background check on her, and her record was squeaky clean. She'd never even had any kind of traffic ticket.

"When is your birthday?" Kyrie asked causing Khelani to smirk.

The getting to know one another questions in the beginning of a man and woman meeting was always sort of comical to her. Most men knew their intentions weren't good and they were going to waste your time, but they still put so much effort into the façade. It was sick. Rather than express these feelings to Kyrie however, she simply answered.

"My birthday is October tenth."

"That's coming up in a few months. You have anything planned?"

"Not at the moment. Holidays aren't really my thing." Kemp had money, and he always spoiled his girls with material possessions, but he wasn't affectionate by far, and her mother was affectionate with who she chose to be affectionate with. Being that she saved all of her praises and love for Anya, Khelani avoided her whenever possible. Her holidays weren't spent with her loving and doting family. Most times, they were spent with her in her room wishing for the day she could leave her parents' home and live on her own.

"Damn. I love holidays. Especially Christmas. Stick with me and we might be wearing matching Christmas pajamas," Kyrie joked.

Khelani shook her head. "I don't think that will ever happen. But it's a good thing that I don't do relationships and that you have trust issues. So, we already know this isn't going very far."

Kyrie had seen women play that hard shit and weeks later, their ass would be behind closed doors begging and crying for him to just love them and do right. He was confident that he had the skills necessary to break down the hardest woman, but her determination had him very interested. It was almost like his own personal challenge to make her ass deviate from all that being against relationships talk.

"I do have trust issues, but I also know that we never know what life holds for us. I believe in just going with the flow. It's not that far-fetched to feel like when we meet the person we're supposed to be with, we'll know, and it will make us change our way of thinking. I don't know what I could be for you or to you unless we give it a try, and the same goes for you. I could end up being the nigga to change your life."

"I doubt it, but I can't knock how you feel."

"So, you're saying I'm wasting my time? I should stop trying to get to know you? You're not interested in dates or seeing where this could go?"

"I'm saying that I don't do relationships, so this could only go so far. I'm also saying that I don't stay in one place for long so after a year no more than two, I'll be ready to move on to another state. My life is very unpredictable right now, but I do know what I won't allow to knock me off track, and that's a man. I have no problem with us being friends or hanging out, but I don't think we need to develop any kind of attachment towards one another, at all."

Kyrie was stunned. Khelani was something else. Most women would be elated that his rich ass was showing interest in them whether they had their own money or not. He was a good damn catch. What single woman was turning him down? He had to respect her wishes though. No matter how confused he was as to why she wasn't falling in his lap vying for his attention, he'd never be pressed. For any woman. Maybe she was gay on the low. Kyrie nodded at her words.

"I have no choice but to respect that."

He wasn't about to be salty, and he was still going to enjoy their outing, so he kept the conversation flowing until they arrived at the restaurant. He continued to open doors for her and treat her the same way he did prior to being shot down. Khelani didn't sugarcoat shit for anyone, but she almost felt bad for the way she handled him.

"You know the way I feel has nothing to do with you, right? You haven't done one thing to rub me the wrong way. My mind was already made up about men way before I met you."

"Who hurt you shorty? We're adults. Let's have a conversation. I'm just curious to know what has you so dead set against ever giving another man a chance? A nigga made a baby on you? Got married on you? What?"

Khelani smirked. If only it had been something so trivial. Once she made a name for herself in Atlanta, there was a huge chance that Kyrie would find out what she did for a living, but she wasn't ready to tell him that just yet. If she couldn't tell him what she did, then she couldn't tell him the real story. Khelani shifted her body in her seat.

"I let my guard down and let a man get close enough to me to attempt to steal from me."

Kyrie's eyes flew to the watch on her wrist. It looked to be worth a few thousand, but what kind of lame ass nigga was going around stealing from women. Khelani appeared to be doing well for sure, but a man had to be super corny to steal from her. "What he took some jewelry or something?"

"He got into my safe and what was inside was far from petty."

That got Kyrie's attention. When he looked over her resume, she had a job history as an office manager. He didn't know too many females or people that had legal money period that kept their money in safes. He wanted to ask so many more questions, but he chose not to. Maybe later. There was something about Khelani and no matter how hard she resisted him, he was going to get to the bottom of who she was as a person.

"So, did you let the nigga explain? Or at least try to?"

"I don't know about you but if I catch a person in my safe, a safe that I didn't give them the code to, there won't be a lot of talking."

Kyrie let out a light chuckle. "So, you beat him up? I'm just saying. Once you were calm, did he try to come back and at least give an explanation?"

"Dead men don't talk."

The ice in her tone, and the fire blazing in Khelani's eyes had him damn near at a loss for words. She said that shit like a real ass gangsta. She killed the nigga? Kyrie's dick almost got hard. It had been confirmed that Khelani wasn't like most at all. It also confirmed his suspicions that she had other shit going on. There had to be something she wasn't telling him. Maybe a ex got locked up or got killed and left her money. He didn't want to come across as being nosey, and he didn't want to overstep his boundaries, so he decided to chill on the questions for a bit.

"My bad gangsta. All jokes aside, someone violated your trust in a major way, and you have every right to be guarded. I have never hit a woman in my life but if I walked in the room and saw a woman in my safe, I might bust her ass that day. I can see why you wouldn't let the average person get close to you but you're letting that fuck nigga win if you deprive yourself of happiness because of what he did. I don't steal, but I'd cut my dick off before I steal from a woman. Shit is lame."

Khelani appreciated his persistence, but she was over it. She wasn't about to keep explaining to Kyrie why she refused to take him serious. More than likely, he didn't want anything deep with her either. He was just letting his ego lead the way. Khelani knew how to choose her battles, so she simply replied with, "You're right."

They finished dinner, and the food was amazingly good. They had just left the restaurant and got back to the car when Kasim called her phone.

"Hey," she answered right away.

"I hate to bother you, but I have bad news. Delante got robbed. He took a bullet to the arm, and the fuck nigga got away with twenty pounds."

Khelani's nostrils flared. It could have been much worse, but she was still livid. "Were you there? Are you okay?"

Kyrie's eyes shot over to Khelani, and he could see that she was pissed.

"I'm fine. I shouldn't have let him go alone, but we had mad people to serve and—"

Khelani cut him off. "Nah, I shouldn't have left. I'm on the next flight home."

Kyrie eyed her with concern. "Everything okay?" he asked when she ended the call.

"Yeah. I just need to go home. I'm sorry. I'll still get my work done."

"No worries mami. I can get my jet to take you as soon as you're ready but are you sure you're okay."

All Khelani could do was nod, but she wasn't okay. She hadn't even been in town three months yet and fuck niggas were trying her already. She needed to get back to Atlanta and make an example out of niggas.

Chapter Ten

Tae counted the money a second time before zipping the bag back up and looking over at Camila. "You know I'm not gon' be able to keep covering for you, right?" He peered into Camila's glassy eyes.

"What you mean?" she attempted to play dumb.

Tae kissed his teeth. "Come on man. The last two times I picked money up for Kyrie, the shit been short. Something tells me you're dipping in the product ma."

Camila tried her best to be offended, but she was so damn zooted, she couldn't have fooled Stevie Wonder. Her eyes were shifty and wild. Kyrie had some good ass coke. It was pure, and Camila was becoming heavily addicted. She was no longer the casual user.

"Nigga, you accusing me of stealing from my blood? And lowkey calling me a coke head?"

Tae grabbed her face with his hand. "Chill with the trying to insult my intelligence ma. I don't give a fuck what you do, 'cus you're grown. You don't have to explain shit to *me*, but

Kyrie isn't about to be looking at me like I keep shorting him. You gotta fix this shit."

The drug in her system and the intensity of the moment, had her heart beating like a drum in her chest. "You know I like that rough shit," a lazy grin eased across her face. Tae's ass was fine. She'd always flirted with Kyrie's friends. Ghalen wasn't the best looking one, but his paper was long. He refused to touch her however, out of loyalty to Kyrie.

Tae though. His fine chocolate ass had her kitty purring at the moment. He had money too, he was sexy, cocky, and aggressive. All of the characteristics that she liked in a man. Anytime she subtly flirted with him, he might simply smirk or say some slick shit back. It never went past that but with the way he was grabbing on her and checking her, had Camila ready to bust it open for him, right there.

Tae peered into her eyes for a bit as he contemplated his next move. It didn't take him long to decide that he wasn't about to let pussy knock him off his square. He needed to get at Kyrie ASAP about this problem. "I have business to handle," was his response as he let Camila's face go.

Tae grabbed the black bag that was on her desk and left the office. As soon as he was in his car and out of the noisy club, he called Kyrie. Tae was glad that Kyrie was a businessman and a smart man. Some people might be quick to take Camila's word over his because she was blood, but Kyrie knew that Camila was a wild card. A wild card that fucked up often.

"Yo, what up?"

"I have a few things to tell you. I found the first thing out right before I pulled up at the club. So, you want the good news first or the bad news?"

"What's the bad news nigga?"

"Money was short again, and Camila tweaking. I think

she's using that shit man. On God, you know I would never steal from you."

There was a brief silence on the other end of the phone while Kyrie beat himself up. Camila was the reason he never wanted daughters. That damn girl was hell. Her snorting coke wasn't a reach at all. He could definitely believe it, and he hated that he even started supplying her ass.

"What's the good news?"

"I found out who the person is that's taking your clientele. Bitch named Khelani."

***

"So, the nigga Snow hit you up for twenty pounds of weed a day after he copped Twelve ounces. Then, you go to serve him, and he doesn't answer the door, but you get robbed on the way back to the car? You already know it was him, right?" Khelani's eyes darted from Kasim to Delante.

"Oh, we know that for sure," Kasim replied. "Problem is we ran up in the crib we met him at and some bitch with a baby was in there. Claimed Snow doesn't live there, and he'd only been there once to drop off a grill that he made for her nigga. If that baby wasn't in there, I would have done her in."

Khelani clenched her jaw muscles. She didn't want unnecessary bloodshed. If she could help it, the only person that would be killed would be the nigga that robbed her. "Nah, no need for all that. We just gon' find out where that nigga be. And this the nigga that Anya put you on to?"

Kasim nodded, and Khelani closed her eyes and blew out a small breath. She couldn't be too mad because Malachi almost robber her ass. Getting close to niggas was just a bad idea period. Anya could be reckless, but she wasn't going to hold this one against her. Khelani pulled out her phone and called Anya's phone."

"Hey," she replied sounding half-asleep.

"Where the fuck that nigga Snow live at?"

Anya's eyes popped open. She was confused because she'd been jarred from her sleep but hearing Snow's name was enough to catch her attention. "Huh? I don't know where he lives. Why? What's wrong?"

"You said he was yo' people, right? He robbed Delante and that's his ass. Where you know him from?"

Anya groaned. Why were people so stupid? He really robbed the person that she put him on to? The dick was superb. So superb in fact, that it was him that had fucked her to sleep. She let him come over since Khelani went away. Something told her to make his ass leave before she went to sleep, and she now was glad she did. And he had the nerve to come smile in her face and have sex with her after he robbed her people? That was scandalous indeed.

"He has a lil' shop where he makes grills. I can look it up and text you the address. I really thought he was cool people. My bad Khelani."

"It's all good Anya. Shit happens. I just hope you don't have any kind of an attachment to this nigga because it's gon' end real bad for him. You know that right?"

"I know." Khelani liked Malachi's ass, and she killed him with no hesitation. Anya hated to see how dirty she would do a nigga that she didn't give a damn about.

Anya didn't allow herself to become too attached to men either because they were always doing dumb shit. They would either get locked up, get themselves killed, cheat, or something. All a man could do for Anya was give her dick and money. If the money and the dick stopped or the dick was trash, she was as good as gone. Mozzy had been calling her so much that she had to end up blocking his little dick ass. She didn't care if she saw him in the club either. Anya had tried to spare him but the next time he bothered her, she was going to let him know that his sex was trash, and she never wanted to fuck him again. If he didn't like it, oh well. She wasn't stroking the ego of a nigga that couldn't even properly stroke her walls.

When Anya got off the phone with Khelani, her thoughts for some reason drifted to Caresha. She was going to be a single mother for real once Snow was dead. Damn. Cold world. Since Anya's sleep had been disturbed, she decided to go ahead and get up for the day. She would get dressed, go get food, and go to the club a little earlier than usual. Anya was all about the money. She had quite a few prospects lined up. Anya decided to hold off a little on dealing with anybody else until they proved for sure, that they were worth it. She knew off the rip that Snow wasn't a baller, but he was sexy, and she just wanted to have some fun. The sex made her glad that she'd given him a chance, but it was too bad that he decided to end his own life by being a cruddy nigga. Mozzy, that nigga was a hot mess for sure, but for a whole different reason.

Anya had been blinded by him always getting sections and bottles and tipping a little money. He worked for a boss ass nigga, but he was far from rich. And even if he was, Anya wouldn't be able to stomach having sex with him again. She had to choose a little more carefully next time. The few guys that she'd been flirting with lately all had ice, and they came into the club with stacks upon stacks of ones. They dressed fly as hell and appeared to be getting it, but Camila put her up on game. Half those niggas were scammers. They cracked credit cards and cashed fraudulent checks. A man could be in the club with mad jewelry on, dripping in designer, ordering plenty bottles and looking like that nigga, and go home to the slums. Some of them didn't even have cars. Just designer clothes, jewelry, and electronics. When Anya thought hard about it, fucking with a scammer might not be too bad if he could use some of those cards to buy her nice things.

A few hours later, Anya was strolling into the club. It wasn't packed at all, but she expected that since she arrived early. She changed clothes and perched on a stool at the bar. She was going to get good and fucked up and hopefully, it would be a good night. Most professional white men didn't frequent the bar after dark. They actually wouldn't be caught dead there but there was one small group of lawyers that let time get away from them. All the beautiful women, the flavorful wings, and the strong drinks had them turned up. Anya was finishing up her first drink, when a blonde haired man walked over to her. She could tell by the lopsided grin on his face that he was drunk as shit.

"You are so fuckin' beautiful," his eyes roamed her body. "Can I get a table dance before I go?"

A big smile graced Anya's face. "You sure can baby." She slid seductively off the stool and followed him back to his table swinging her hips every step of the way.

The man's friends all looked on in amazement at the woman that he picked, and Anya wasted no time getting down to business. She twerked, gyrated on laps while rubbing on herself, and gave all of the men a hell of a show. They were tossing money at her and by the time they left, she had $395 in her possession. Anya smiled and mumbled to herself. "I knew it was going to be a good ass night."

After heading over to the bar, she ordered another drink. Business was still kind of slow, but the night was young. She laughed and talked with a few other strippers and patrons of the club but when she saw Mozzy, her mood was instantly ruined. His ass was like a fuckin' fly. Why wouldn't he just go away? Anya decided to head to the back to get out his view. Just knowing he was near was killing her vibe, but she didn't move fast enough. She had just stood up, when he grabbed her arm.

"Where you going, Love? I'm trying to get a dance."

"I have to go to the bathroom," Anya gave him a fake smile while resisting the urge to roll her eyes. The cologne he wore smelled pricy. He was dressed nice, and she still wanted no parts of him. Funny how bad sex from a nigga could make you look at him completely different.

"Nah. I want my dance. It's not gon' take long, and we both know you like to ignore muhfuckas. Damn my money not good enough for you no more?"

Anya was over it. The alcohol and the agitation she was feeling from his persistence didn't mix. "Look, take a hint bruh. Got damn. You don't have to be a pest. You were cool and all, but I'm not feeling it. Stop calling me. Stop texting me. You don't have to tip me when you come in here. There are plenty of females to entertain you. Leave me the hell alone. Aight?" she snapped.

The smile that eased across Mozzy's face contradicted the anger blazing in his eyes. He was giving off weird ass energy, and Anya wanted to be away from him. Just as she snatched her arm away from him, he eased his gun out of the pocket of the thin jacket that he wore. "Working for Kyrie has its' perks. Security lets me in with this bad boy right here. Now, follow me to my section or get dragged outside and eat a bullet. Your choice."

Anya's heart slammed into her chest. He was doing all this because she rejected him? Nigga was corny as fuck, and she hated the night she ever left the club with him. Camila's ass was right about him, and she was too damn dumb and stubborn to listen. Anya contemplated making a run for it, but she didn't know just how deep Kyrie's reach went. If the bouncers let him in with a gun on the strength of Kyrie, they might not stop him from dragging her out of the club. They might think he was her nigga or some shit. She would go do the dance for him, then she'd let security and Camila know that either he couldn't come back in the club, or she was going elsewhere to dance.

Reluctantly, Anya followed Mozzy to the section. His ass came in the club several times a week getting sections and tipping strippers. Meanwhile, his lame ass was living at a hotel. Mozzy sat down, and Anya began to dance in front of him. Since her back was to his, she didn't even notice him unzipping his jeans or pulling his penis through the slit. His perverted ass didn't even care that he was pulling his dick out in a strip club.

With lightening speed, he grabbed Anya and forced her into his lap. He put one hand around her neck from behind and choked her, while pulling her thong to the side with the other hand. His grip on her neck was so tight, that Anya couldn't scream or get up off his lap. His dick was so damn little that even him forcing his way into her middle while she wasn't aroused didn't even hurt her. Anya just felt disgusted and violated, and tears sprang to her eyes. She'd done a lot of shit. In her eyes, she was wild. You only live once, and she was nowhere near as reserved as Khelani, but being raped had her fucked up. Mozzy choked her while scooting to the edge of his seat and pumping in and out of her. She was tight and warm and despite the act not being consensual, her body betrayed her. Anya began to get wet, and Mozzy was in heaven. At times, his grip would loosen a little on her neck, and then it would tighten back up. He didn't last long in the pussy but by the time he came, she had begun to feel as if she was about to pass out. Her lips even had a blue tinge to them.

Mozzy pushed her off his lap, and Anya fell to the floor. She struggled to breathe, and she was dizzy, so it took her a minute to get up off the floor. Camila walked by and saw Anya on the floor. She also saw Mozzy breathing hard and zipping his jeans back up. Her eyes darted from him to Anya, and her eyes narrowed as she peeped that Anya's lips were blue, and tears ran down her cheeks.

"What the fuck is going on in here?"

Anya peeled herself up off the floor. Fuck Kyrie's pull. Even if she had to get Kasim to get at Mozzy, he was going to pay for what he just did. "He fuckin' raped me," Anya cried in a shaky voice.

Camila's eyes flew over to Mozzy, and he kissed his teeth. "That bitch is fuckin' lying. Why would I have to rape her when I've fucked her before? She's just a freak. She pulled my shit out and started riding it."

Anya's voice was raspy from being choked, and there were marks on her neck. It was easy to see who was telling the truth. "Nigga, why are her lips blue? Why are there marks on her neck? Why was she on the floor?"

Mozzy shrugged passively. "She a freak. Bitch likes when I choke her."

"I told her the night she left with you that you were a broke ass lame." That comment wiped the smirk off Mozzy's face. "You're pathetic as hell. You might be seeing a little bread from being Kyrie's do boy, but you're still corny in my eyes."

Camila's comment infuriated Mozzy so much so that he took a step towards her. "You better watch how you talk to me bitch. Don't get fucked up trying to handle me."

Camila let out a snort. "Nigga please. Kyrie made ya bum ass and one phone call to him, and he'll end ya bum ass. Get the fuck out of my club."

Her comment made Mozzy so mad that his upper lip twitched. He was two seconds away from knocking her out, but he had to remember who she was. He was in this city, and he had the money that he had thanks to Kyrie. He was still driving the rental that Kyrie paid for and still living in the hotel that he foot the bill for. If he wasn't trying to go back to Houston with his tail tucked between his legs, he had to put his pride to the side and leave. It took every ounce of self-restraint that he had, but he walked away.

Camila looked over at Anya. She knew nothing good would come of her dealing with Mozzy, but she had to learn the hard way. "You going to the hospital so they can do a rape kit?"

Anya was so shaken up that she was trembling. "No. They'll call the police, and I don't want that."

"Just go ahead and leave for the night. Get yourself together. You'll be okay. Don't let that fuck nigga break you. I'll get Arman to make sure he leaves." That was as deep as her pep talk went. Camila wasn't a very affectionate person. Anya was a tough girl, and Camila felt like she'd be okay.

Anya nodded and walked towards the dressing room. It literally felt as if bugs were crawling on her skin. She wanted to go home and scrub her skin off. If it was the last thing she did, Anya was going to make Mozzy pay for what he did to her.

Chapter Eleven

Kyrie sat on the edge of his desk waiting for the knock to come. He had been waiting for this shit all day. When he found out that Khelani sold weed, he wasn't the least bit shocked. In fact, everything about it made sense. It would be hard for him to go all day at work without confronting her, so he didn't go into the office until later. Kyrie played different events over and over in his mind. Like her speaking on the nigga that she caught in her safe and saying he was no longer alive. Anyone could look at her and tell she had her own money. Even her saying that she never stayed in one place for long. It was all adding up now. This entire time, he'd been smiling in the face of the person that came in town and started taking his clientele. Kyrie didn't like feeling played. If she had some fire ass weed that she was moving like that, she didn't need to work for him. Unless she had a motive. Yet, her ass was always the one talking about how she didn't trust people. The more he thought about it, it made his blood boil.

He didn't go into the record label until four pm. Most

everyone left for the day at 5. Including Khelani. "Come to my office before you leave," he instructed her before going into his office and closing the door.

When she knocked, the anxiety he felt heightened. "Come in."

Khelani walked in dressed in a snakeskin print dress that had thin straps and stopped at her knees. Underneath the dress, she wore a crème turtleneck sweater, and on her feet were black thigh high boots. Khelani had a very unique sense of fashion, and she could be a stylist for sure. Even in his anger, Kyrie had to stop and respect her fashion sense. He quickly recovered though.

"I got niggas telling me that they've copped some pretty good weed from you. Seems like you just appeared out of thin air and started snatching up my clientele. So, all that bullshit you spat about being an asset to my company was game, huh? You started working here to get close to me for what? To take my customers?" He didn't even know her that well, but he felt betrayed. He let that shy girl, good girl, classy bitch act, knock him off his square.

"I had no way of knowing who your clientele is or was. I deal with about nine people here in Atlanta. I did start working here to make the right connections in the city. Any of your clientele that came to me was a coincidence."

She didn't appear to be lying. She looked him in the eye as she spoke, and she appeared confident. Kyrie was still pissed though. "Who the fuck are you?"

"As I told you before, I'm from Trinidad. My father sent me to the states to start a pipeline for him back to Trinidad. He's the plug there. I set up shop in Charlotte, and Atlanta was my next stop."

Kyrie let out a brief chuckle. "So, you like a got damn

queen pen or some shit, huh? You get up every day and come in this bitch and work hard like you need this lil' money. You're smart for sure. A woman that will do anything to get what she wants." His eyes bore into hers as he spoke.

"Kyrie, I came to Atlanta to sell weed. I didn't come with malicious intent or some kind of vendetta against you. I'm new in town, and it made sense to me to get on at the label and make connections. I'm sorry if you feel deceived. I did my job and so far, I haven't even made any useful connections. I'm used to dealing with the big fish, and it's obvious that your clientele likes what I have. You could cop your weed from me and go back to serving them."

What she said made sense, but that didn't stop Kyrie from being livid. "I guess it's safe to say that you no longer work here." He refused to acknowledge what she said about him buying weed from her. His ego was wounded, and Khelani could see that clear as day.

"Okay." She removed her badge from the strap of her dress and placed it on her desk. "I can go log out of my computer and get my things."

Kyrie damn near felt panicked. Even in his anger, he didn't want her to walk out of that door. He was surprised that for as upset as he was, he didn't want to see her go. His emotions were all over the place, and that only added to his anger. What kind of hold did this woman have over him?

"Nah. As a matter of fact, you can work for the next two weeks. You leaving now will put Kim in a bind."

Khelani poked the inside of her jaw with her tongue in an effort to compose herself. She was done trying to stroke Kyrie's bruised ego. He had her fucked up. "So, I'm not sure what you think this is, but you don't snap your fingers and I just do what you want me to do. Now, I can work from home for a few days while Kim looks for a replacement. After that, you're on your own."

Kyrie stood up. "If you were anybody else, you might just get robbed of the work that you have and sent back to wherever you came from," his upper lip curled slightly.

Khelani cocked her head to the left and studied him a bit. "You run a multi-million dollar company, and you're crying because you lost a few niggas that don't even cop more than two or three pounds at a time? You're doing all this for what? You'd risk your career and your life by robbing me 'cus don't think shit is sweet just because I'm a female. My father runs Trinidad, and his reach is long. Remember that shit. You mad because you wined and dined me, and you never got the pussy? I didn't fall at your feet and submit. Shit didn't go how you planned, and you're salty?"

"I get it. You must be a dyke. You wear the strap when you fuck bitches?"

Khelani smirked at Kyrie. "I take dick very well. Is that the issue Kyrie? You want to fuck? Just say that then, and maybe we can work something out."

Kyrie wanted to say fuck her. He wanted to tell her to get out of his office and to stay away from his clientele, but the bulge in his jeans gave way to his true feelings. In a matter of seconds, his dick was so hard that it hurt. He wanted to wipe the smirk off her face. Invading her personal space, Kyrie walked up on her gently pushing her body with his.

"I think you're getting a kick out of playing with me. You might want to find you something safe to do ma."

When Khelani didn't respond, Kyrie placed one hand around her neck as if he was choking her. Squeezing gently, he placed his lips on hers and snaked his tongue in her mouth. She smelled sweet, and her mouth tasted sweeter. It was what Kyrie had been craving, and he was determined to make her fold. His hand made its' way up her skirt and ripped the red lace panties that she wore. Their kiss deepened as he fumbled with his belt buckle and freed his dick from his Marc Jacob boxer briefs.

Kyrie hoisted Khelani up, and she wrapped her legs around his waist. Staring into her face, he pressed the head of his dick at her opening, and she was already juicy for him. Crossing that line with Khelani might prove to be a mistake, but the sexual chemistry between them so was thick that it was damn near choking him. He pushed into her a little more, and she clenched her pussy muscles around the part of him that was in her. Yes, she was dangerous indeed, but Kyrie was determined to get some kind of reaction out of her. He pushed himself deeper into her, and it was his turn to smirk when her face crumpled slightly, and her mouth fell open. He had her ass.

With her back pressed against the wall and her legs locked around his body, Kyrie stirred Khelani's middle with passion and aggression. He was fucking her like a man just released from prison. Since he couldn't get to her breasts because of the outfit that she wore, his lips found hers again, and their tongues did a sensual dance. Khelani moaned in his mouth, and that shit turned him on. She wrapped her arms around his neck, and he carried her over to his desk. After sitting her down, he pulled back and bit and bit his bottom lip as he watched his dick slide in and out her of pink treasure. She was so wet that her essence made his dick look glazed. He used his thumb to gently stroke her clit as he continued to massage the walls of her pussy, and Khelani let out a long moan.

Kyrie pulled all the way out of her and peered into her eyes as he used his dick to lightly beat her clit. He slid his dick up and down her slit, and Khelani lifted her hips slightly. She wanted him back inside of her. He watched her as she licked her lips.

"You want this dick?"

He was about to piss her off. Kyrie's ego trip was interrupting her impending orgasm. Just like a man to want his ego stroked at the worst time. Khelani had always been the stubborn one so rather than answering, she just narrowed her eyes into slits and peered at him. Kyrie chuckled. Her defiance was cute, but he wasn't willing to give up.

"Tell me you want this dick."

Khelani almost got up and told him to fuck himself, but Kasim's words echoed through her mind. *"You're too powerful, Khelani. You'll never find a man unless you submit. No man can take you outshining him."*

If he wanted to play, she could play too. "I want that dick. Please give it to me, baby," she moaned and had to stifle her laughter at the shock that registered on Kyrie's face. He hadn't even expected her to give in and say the shit.

"Kyrie baby, please," she repeated, and that was all she wrote.

Kyrie slid back into her with a savage groan and went back to assaulting her pussy. The office was empty, and Kehani was glad because when waves of pleasure ripped through her body from an orgasm so intense that it made her toes curl, she cried out in pure ecstasy. She'd never had such an intense orgasm. It left her body trembling and jerking, and it didn't help that Kyrie hadn't eased his strokes up. His balls slapped against her pussy as he gritted his teeth and tried to fuck the taste out of her mouth. The orgasm made her already soaked pussy wet beyond belief, and it was hard for Kyrie to hold off on his own nut. In fact, her pussy was so good and had him in such a zone, that he didn't even pull out. Kyrie groaned as he came inside her with not one regret in the world.

A thin layer of sweat decorated her upper lip, and she looked so beautiful that Kyrie forgot about the slight power trip. With his dick still inside of her, he leaned down so that they were chest to chest and placed a juicy kiss on her lips. They locked eyes for a moment. Just for that moment, it was as if time stood still. Nothing else mattered, and the only people that existed were them. It didn't take long for either of them to snap back to reality. Kyrie slid out of her, and Khelani stood up. Her panties were ruined, so she stepped out of them and put them in the trash. Without speaking a word, she headed out of Kyrie's office and headed to the bathroom to clean herself off. All he could do was stare after her.

"Muhfuckin' Khelani."

"WHAT ARE YOU DOING HERE?" Anya asked as she headed into the kitchen and saw Khelani sitting on the couch holding her laptop.

"I live here."

"Ha ha. Why aren't you at work? Anya tried to mask her agitation. She wanted to smoke, drink, and forget her sorrows. Who cared if it wasn't even noon? The rape she endured at the hands of Mozzy was still heavy on her mind, and she wanted to numb herself. Anya was a grown ass woman, but she didn't feel like having Khelani looking down on her and judging her if she got shit faced early in the day.

"I'm working from home. My cover is blown. Kyrie found out that I'm the person that's been taking some of his clientele, and he wasn't too happy about it. I told him he should get on the money train, but I don't think his pride will allow him to cop from a girl."

Anya looked over her shoulder. "Damn. He probably thought you were some low-level chick that would be impressed by what he has only to find out that you don't do too bad for yourself. Nigga would rather eat crow than cop his shit from you," she chortled.

Khelani sighed. "I know. I shouldn't even be helping his ass, but I'm doing it for Kim. Nigga fired me then said, nah you're gonna help Kim. I had to check him on that shit real fast. I know I threatened his manhood and all, but he had me fucked up."

"I'm sure. He was trying to wine and dine you and impress you, then he finds out you're not who he thought you was. But I mean, now that the cover is blown, why not let loose. Why not give dating him a try? I know he'd still be open to it because if he didn't like you, he wouldn't be tripping so hard. Kyrie is supposed to be about his paper. You come into town with some fire ass weed and he's not trying to buy you out? That's his ego for sure."

"Because I don't want to date him. I don't want to date anybody. I just killed the man that I was dating less than three months ago. I think I need to get over that first."

Anya kissed her teeth. "You liked Malachi, but you didn't love him. And the moment you saw him in your safe, any feelings you had for him disappeared. I know you. Been around you every day of my life for my entire life. The moment Kasim disposed of that nigga's body, he no longer existed to you. You're not hurt."

Khelani rolled her eyes upward. "Okay I have work to do, and you're distracting me." Anya didn't take anything serious. Not even her own life, but here she was trying to read Khelani. It was almost comical.

Khelani didn't love Malachi. She never claimed too, but the sting of his betrayal didn't hurt any less. Khelani had no desire to ever again let her guard down and be disappointed by a man. Kyrie was rich, handsome, and very charming. To fall for him would be signing up to forever be in competition with the many females that wanted to be with him. Falling for him would mean trusting him to be committed to her and not sleep around, and Khelani would drink glass before she trusted a man to be faithful. Too much came with dealing with a man. It could never just be easy and fun. It might start out that way but at some point, it would switch up. Someone would catch feelings, and the entire dynamic of the relationship would change. Plus, she moved around too much. Khelani didn't have time to be invested in one man but...

Every time she thought back to their escapade in his office, her pussy throbbed. Khelani thought she'd had sex enough times in her life to be considered sexually experienced, but Kyrie showed her what she'd been missing. It was the absolute best sexual experience that she'd had in her life. The first orgasm she ever had was with Malachi, and he didn't even make her cum every time they had sex. She didn't cum with him until the fifth or sixth time they had fucked, and she was very comfortable with him. He made her have an orgasm a total of two times before she found him attempting to rob her and killed him. Everything about Kyrie did it for her. The passion behind his kisses, the intensity of his gazes, the aggressive yet gentle way that he handled her. It sent chills down her spine in a good way.

She pushed thoughts of Kyrie from her mind and went back to work. Knowing that her job with his label would be over in a few days made her feel a sense of relief, but she was a little sad also. Although it was tiring, Khelani felt normal getting dressed everyday in her cute little outfits and going to work. She enjoyed being in the presence of and having conversations with people other than Kasim and Anya. It was secretly nice to have Kyrie pining for her, even though she knew they'd never go anywhere. Khelani wondered what it would be like to pull an Anya move and tell her father that she no longer wanted to work for him. What if she just got a regular job and lived a regular life? She had enough money for a hefty down payment on a home. Her beamer was paid for and even if she put money down on a house, she'd be left with enough money to have a nice cushion for a few years. She could for sure make it working a regular job. Khelani once again took a mental break from her work and daydreamed. What would she do if she wasn't selling drugs?

She loved fashion and could see herself being a stylist. Khelani was jarred from her daydream when she got a text message alert. After picking up her phone, she saw that Kyrie had sent her a message that simply said: **Let's talk numbers**.

Khelani placed her laptop on the couch and got up to go get her burner phone. She didn't talk business on her iPhone. With baited breath, she called Kyrie and waited for him to answer.

"This is my business phone. What were you looking to cop?"

"I already know it's good because niggas are going crazy for it, so let me start with a Hundred pounds and we will see where it goes from there."

"I can arrange that. How soon would you like to get them? I can send my right hand Kasim to se—"

"Nah," Kyrie cut her off abruptly. "I'm only dealing with you."

Khelani breathed in deeply through her nose. Kyrie and his stubbornness was starting to irritate her. He was acting like a big ass baby. If he wanted to see her, he could just say that instead of making demands. She was going to appease him, however. He was trying to cop a hundred pounds and unlike him, she wasn't going to let emotions get in the way of money.

"When do you want to meet Kyrie?"

"My place this evening. I'll text you the address. Does 7 pm work for you?"

Now he was trying to be accommodating. "It does."

"Cool."

He ended the call without another word, and all Khelani could do was shake her head.

Chapter Twelve

Kyrie headed into the club knowing that shit wasn't going to go well. He'd been busy and had so much going on that he hadn't been able to confront Camila about what he was told, but today was the day. He nodded his head in the direction of anyone that spoke to him, but he was a man on a mission. He headed straight into the office and found Camila sitting at the desk scrolling through her phone. The first thing he noticed was that when she looked up at him, she looked a little flushed, but a sense of relief crossed her face almost immediately.

"'Bout time. You got that? One of the strippers hit me up twice already. She has regular customers that come in and cop."

"I'm not giving you any more coke, Camila."

You didn't sell drugs for as long as Kyrie had and not pick up on the traits and habits of users. Camila was antsy. She wanted more coke, and it wasn't to make money off of.

"Why not? Is it because of dad? I told you he's not going to find out."

"It has nothing to do with him. When I picked the money

up a few weeks ago, it was $200 short, and I didn't say shit because you're family. The first time Tae picked it up, it was $500 short. Last time, it was $1300 short. You not about to keep stealing from me and thinking shit is sweet. On top of that, it's not like you're just stealing. You're using the shit, Camila." Had she not been so livid, she would have seen the pain in her cousin's eyes. She'd done a lot of shit to disappoint him, but this took the cake.

"I'm not using shit. You keep listening to Tae. That nigga don't know me," Camila hissed. "Maybe ya man is stealing from you, but don't put that shit on me."

Kyrie shook his head. "You're dangerous shawty. You know how I get down, and you know that if I really thought Tae was stealing from me, I'd hurt that man. You're my blood, and I love you, but I'm gon' distance myself from you for a bit. You need to get your mind right."

It felt to Camila like Kyrie was being mean to her, but his words to her caused an ache in his heart. Cutting her off would be like cutting off his sister, but she was going to stand in his face and blame Tae for some shit that she knew she did. It didn't get any worse than that. Camila did too much. Often, and it had to come to an end. He couldn't keep entertaining her shit or enabling her. It was time for her to grow up.

"Distance yourself from me?" she snatched her head back. "You're acting real brand new right now, Kyrie. You want me to give you the lil' petty ass two grand? Your rich ass is acting like you were missing some serious stacks."

"It's not about the amount; it's about the principal. That attitude right there is why I can't fuck with you. I don't need you to wash my money anymore. I'll handle the shit myself. You be easy." Kyrie left the office leaving Camila fuming.

She knew plenty of niggas that she could get coke from, but she wanted Kyrie's shit. She grabbed her purse and left her office to go and get some before the club started getting too packed. On her way out, she saw Anya and Snow conversing at the bar, and her eyes narrowed into slits. That was one hoe ass bitch. She'd just been raped by Mozzy, and here she was all up in Snow's face. Camila had no idea that Anya was confronting Snow about robbing her people. He was playing dumb, but Anya knew better.

Camila's skin felt clammy as she headed for the door. She would deal with Anya and Snow another time. No one knew but her that her being so against Anya and Snow had nothing to do with her loyalty to Caresha. She'd fucked Snow a few times herself. The last time in fact, had been a month ago and like Anya, she was hooked on the dick. Snow was a professional pipe layer. That's why Caresha's mouth was tore slam off her face. On one coke induced night, Camila took it too far, and she had the best sex of her life with Snow. She felt guilty the next day, and she promised herself she wouldn't do it again. Until she got horny, and he was the only man she wanted. The more they slept together, the more addicted she became. Seeing Snow make googly eyes at Anya burned her ass up because she knew that her and Snow could never be. Caresha would kill her if she ever found out about them.

Being that Caresha was on her mind, it really startled Camila when she walked out of the club and saw Caresha heading towards the entrance looking furious. Camila forgot all about her quest for coke.

"What's wrong with you?"

"I went through that bastard's phone. He's fucking that bitch! You bringing bitches around my nigga, and they fuckin' him?"

"Hold up now Caresha. You already know how Snow is. I told her he was off limits. You act like I hooked them up. I went to go get my grills, and she was with me."

"Well, I'm about to beat her ass."

"I'll tell her to come outside. Don't cause a scene in the club but if she wants to be bold enough to fuck your man, then whoop her ass," Camila said simply. She was agitated that she could no longer sell coke out of the club, she was agitated that Kyrie was pissed with her, and she was agitated that Snow was all up in Anya's face. All of those things were a recipe for disaster. Camila was like a ticking time bomb, and she wasn't anybody's friend. Not Anya's and not Caresha's.

Camila stepped inside the club and saw Snow walking away from Anya. She smirked before calling Anya's name.

"Yo Anya. I need you to step outside for a minute."

Anya didn't second guess Camila's request. She followed Snow, and he stopped dead in his tracks upon seeing Caresha, but she didn't say one word to him. She had beef with one person at the moment and that was Anya. Camila folded her arms underneath her breasts and watched the scene that was about to unfold.

Anya looked confused as Caresha stepped in her face.

"You want to come in my shop smiling in my face and then fuck my nigga, bitch?"

Caresha didn't even give Anya time to answer. She stole off on her causing Anya to stumble since she had on six inch heels. Before Anya could recover, Caresha began raining blows down on her. Jealousy and rage overtook Camila's body, and she jumped in the fight. She was looking like the devoted friend, but she had her own motives. There was no way Anya could get to her feet with both women attacking her, so she curled into a fetal position until the fight was broken up. Snow pulled Caresha off Anya while one of the security guards grabbed Camila. They knew it was bad when blood began to stain the pavement. Anya got up slowly, and her nose and mouth were leaking blood along with a gash in her forehead. Her left eye was already beginning to swell. No matter how much pain she was in, Anya wouldn't let them see her shed one tear.

"You bitches had to jump me? Word? Camila on God next time I see you, I'm doing you dirty."

"Yeah yeah bitch, just grab ya shit and kick rocks."

Camila was mad at the world. In that moment, it was fuck Anya and fuck everybody.

"This shit look like some fire," Kyrie inspected the weed that Khelani had brought into his home. He began to open one of the packages. Glancing up at her, his dick jumped at the sight of her. "Have a seat. Smoke one with me, or are you in a rush?"

Khelani remained standing. "Because you decided to purchase weed from me that erases our entire conversation from yesterday? We just act like none of it ever happened."

"Yeah. Just like we acted like it never happened when I was sliding dick up in you," Kyrie spoke as he pulled buds from the package.

Khelani could only shake her head. This man was something else. When she still didn't sit down, Kyrie stood up and walked over to her. He grabbed each side of her waist as he invaded her personal space.

"All that hard shit is about to stop. You need that wall up when you out dealing with them niggas on your money shit. With me, you calm that shit down. You don't want a relationship, then so be it. You're not going to stay in the A forever, then that's what it is. But while you are here, we gon' do what we do, and you can stop fighting me on that shit."

Khelani didn't respond because the way he checked her made her pussy ache for him. And little did he know, she was tired of fighting him. Exhausted. When she didn't protest, Kyrie dipped his head and found her lips with his.

"You gon' act right?" he spoke into her mouth.

"Ummmhmmm," she moaned as he placed his face in the crook of her neck. All she could think about was having more bomb ass sex with him, and that was enough to make her submit even if it was only temporary.

Pleased with her response, Kyrie pulled back with a smile. "Good. Now, sit down so we can smoke. You hungry? I can get my chef to come through. He lives in this neighborhood."

"I mean I could eat, but how are you going to call him on such short notice?"

"Because I'm that nigga. You let me worry about that." Kyrie picked up his phone from the cup holder of his leather recliner and shot his chef a text. He even told him that if he was available to come by on such short notice, he'd tip him an extra $300.

The duo sat in silence while Kyrie rolled the blunt. As soon as he lit it and took a long pull, his nostrils flared, and he damn near coughed. "Got damn. This shit is like that for real." He took a few more puffs then passed it to Khelani. He hated how into her he was. "Yo' ass had me hotter than fish grease yesterday," he shook his head at the memory.

"I apologize for that. That wasn't my intention. I'm just about my money."

The weed had Kyrie feeling real mellow. "I like that shit," he stated in a low voice. "You just being easy and not giving a nigga a hard time. I'd give ya ass the world if you knew how to act," he chuckled, but he was serious.

Khelani exhaled weed smoke from her lungs. "I can give myself the world."

Kyrie kissed his teeth. "That's the shit I'm talking about. You can but why would you want to? You have a nigga that would do it for you. That shit is crazy as hell to me, but I have to respect who you are because plenty women damn near begged me to settle down with them. They weren't who I wanted though, so I gave them every excuse in the book. Guess that's the game you're playing with me, but it's all good though. If you don't want me, that's what it is."

Khelani was high, and the last thing she wanted was deep conversations. She passed him the blunt back.

"I'm gonna head out." She stood up, and he was right behind her.

"Fuck that Khelani. Fuck all that running and all that tough shit. Got damn just tell me what's good. You don't want me?"

Good dick will make a woman emotional. That and all the shit she had going on was weighing heavily on her. Kyrie didn't know how bad she wanted to just chill out and be a woman. Not a damn drug dealer.

"In another life Kyrie, I wouldn't want anybody but you," she confessed with tear filled eyes. She couldn't believe this nigga had her about to cry.

Her vulnerability made Kyrie want her even more, and he cupped her chin in his hand. "We don't need another life when we have this one." He kissed the corner of her mouth, her nose, her forehead, and then her lips. Khelani's body relaxed as he began to suck softly on her neck.

He moved his mouth back up and spoke against her ear. "I wanna give you all this dick." Kyrie pressed his body into hers, and Khelani felt his erection. That turned her on, but his words made her giggle. "You gon' let me give it to you?"

He pulled back so he could look her in the face, and Khelani simply nodded. That was all he needed to see. Kyrie picked her up and with her legs wrapped around his body and his hands on her ass, he carried her up the stairs to his bedroom. Kyrie took off Khelani's Louis Vuitton combat boots then peeled her black leggings and panties down her thick thighs. After placing his head in between her legs, the scent of cocoa butter on her skin filled his nostrils. Kyrie kissed her clit softly before French kissing it passionately. Khelani's back arched, and she bit her bottom lip as he probed her most sensitive parts with his mouth. When he moaned into her pussy, her body jerked slightly, and Khelani grabbed his curls as he devoured her. The things Kyrie were doing to her pussy with his mouth, had her juices running down the crack of her ass.

Kyrie had a point to prove. He was that nigga, and he often made women fall before they got the D. Once they did get the D however, it was usually a wrap. He'd be ducking and dodging them like crazy, but he welcomed the antics from Khelani. Making her act as if she gave a damn would be the ultimate pleasure for him. It was funny how the right woman could make a man change how he acted and how he moved in general. All he wanted to do was win Khelani over. He knew once he had her, she wasn't going anywhere. The feeling of an impending orgasm engulfed her, and Khelani was desperate to reach that peak. She began thrusting her hips and riding Kyrie's face until her clit swelled, and her pussy began to contract violently. Kyrie didn't let up off her, and he slurped her dry as she moaned and called his name.

He finally came up for air and their tongues connected. Khelani tasted her juices off his lips. Kyrie's beard glistened with her essence, and she played in his hair while her body yearned for him. When Kyrie stood up to undress, Khelani sat up and took her shirt and bra off. They didn't use a condom the first time they had sex, and one wasn't on his mind the second time. Kyrie wasted no time guiding his dick to her opening and easing into her. Khelani let out a shaky breath as he filled her up. Kyrie was too rich to be going around having unprotected sex. He didn't need a bunch of babies to pay for or any STD's to get rid of. If he hit a woman raw, it needed to be understood that the pussy was for him and only him. He didn't feel the need to express his feelings because he doubted Khelani's difficult ass was fucking anybody else.

"That shit feel good?" he asked in a low voice before pecking her on the lips. He knew it did from the way her face was contorted, but he wanted to hear the words.

"It feels very good," she replied as he stirred her middle.

"I want this shit from the back. I want to see that fat ass jiggle while I fuck the shit out of you."

Kyrie pulled out of Khelani, and she got into the doggystyle position. Kyrie spread her round ass cheeks and began eating her out again. Khelani was losing her mind, and that shit stroked the hell out of his ego.

"Fuuccckkkk," Khelani squealed as he pulled out of her and smacked her on the ass hard as hell.

As soon as he slid back into her, she came again. She squirted just a bit and the puddle that appeared on his bed along with the cum that shot onto his stomach and balls made him fuck her savagely. Her reaction to him was turning him on like a muhfucka. The wetter and tighter she became, the better it was for him. Kyrie felt it was safe to say that Khelani had the best pussy he'd ever had. He clenched his teeth together as he pounded in and out of her.

"This my got damn pussy," he roared as he shot his load into her womb. He stayed inside of her for a moment before easing out of her. Kyrie admired her glistening pussy before she got off the bed.

"Where's the bathroom?"

He eyed her naked body and licked his lips. "You heard what I said? That's my pussy."

Khelani smirked. "I heard you loud and clear."

Her and Kyrie engaged in a brief stare down. It would

always be a battle of the egos with them but if Khelani didn't learn anything else from her mother, she learned when to let a man shine. "As long as you act like this, it's yours. But how fair would it be for my pussy to be yours, while your dick is roaming?"

"If it ain't you, fuck a bitch," he replied adamantly making her blush.

"I hear you."

That satisfied him, and he kissed her before leading her to the bathroom. They had just cleaned up and put their clothes back on when Kyrie's chef rang his doorbell. He let Mike in just as Kasim was calling Khelani.

"Hello?"

"I know where that nigga Snow is. He finally went to his shop. Me and Delante are about to run in and fire his ass up."

"Damn, I wanted to be there," Khelani stated, but she knew they didn't have time to wait for her.

"There's no need for you to be here. We got this," Kasim assured her. He was overprotective of Khelani and never wanted her in harm's way.

"Okay. Be careful."

Kyrie's eyes shot in her direction. "Everything good?"

"Yeah. My right hand is just going to handle some shit, and I want to be there."

The way she bit her bottom lip was sexy, and Kyrie had learned her well enough to know that she was conflicted about something. He wasn't sure what the call was about, but he knew the kind of shit Khelani dealt in. If she was his girl, that shit would come to an end ASAP. He knew he couldn't tell her shit though. They were only fucking. Khelani and Kyrie finished smoking the blunt he rolled while Mike prepared seafood pasta, garlic bread, and lamb chops. When they were done eating, she was stuffed and ready to be alone so she could talk to Kasim.

"I have to get going but thank you for dinner. It was delicious."

Kyrie wished he could have gone to bed with her and woke her up the next morning by sliding dick in her.

"You're welcome. Let me know when you make it in the house."

"Will do." She turned to walk away, and he pulled her back. Kyrie didn't let her leave him until he'd placed a few pecks on her lips.

Khelani headed to her car feeling as if she was walking on a cloud. Kyrie made her feel things she didn't want to feel. If she could feel like this every day, he might be worth risking it all for, but this feeling was temporary. After the honeymoon phase came the bullshit. Khelani decided to stay in the moment and not think too much about the future and in the moment, she needed to go get a plan B pill. Khelani couldn't afford any slip ups.

Chapter Thirteen

"What in the fuck happened to your face?!" Khelani asked Anya the next morning. Even though her and Kyrie were on good terms, she was still going to work from home. When Khelani walked into the kitchen for her morning coffee and saw the gruesome sight of her sister's face, her heart dropped into her stomach.

Anya's eye was swollen shut, and there was a gash on her forehead. Her lips were swollen, and she looked as if she'd been beaten mercilessly, and all Khelani saw was red. Anya dropped her head shamefully. The only way she'd been able to get to sleep the night before was to drink tequila until she was damn near sick. She needed something for the pain, but Anya didn't want to go to the hospital.

"Camila and her friend Caresha jumped me," she mumbled as she grabbed ice for her lips. "I was fucking around with Caresha's ex, Snow. They jumped me at the club."

It literally felt like Khelani's blood was boiling. She was furious. "Do you know where these bitches lives?"

Anya could almost feel the heat radiating off her sister. She knew that when Khelani got like this, there was no talking her down, and Anya didn't care. Camila's ass deserved whatever she had coming her weak ass way. Jumping her was some coward ass shit to do. As soon as her face healed, that bitch had to see her. And so was Caresha.

"I've never been to her place. The bitch Caresha works in the same building that Snow does."

"She jumped your ass over a dead nigga because Kasim and Delante handled that nigga last night. I'll let that bitch grieve for a few days before I get her, but I'm on Camila's ass. Today."

Anya knew she wasn't bullshitting. If it wouldn't have hurt so bad, she would have smiled knowing Camila was going to get hers. It also made her feel good to know that Caresha was somewhere crying her eyes out. She didn't feel bad because Snow shouldn't have robbed Delante. He did that shit to himself. Anyone that thought Khelani, Kasim, or Delante were sweet, would be in for a rude awakening every time they tried one of them.

"Do you have something for pain?" Anya asked her sister.

"I'll check in my room."

Khelani wasn't even going to give Anya any lectures about being smart and leaving bitches' niggas alone. No matter who she had sex with, she didn't deserve to be attacked like that by a coward and her friend. They should have fought straight up. Camila didn't have to involve herself, and now she had to see Khelani. As Khelani passed the pain pills to Anya, her phone rang, and she saw that her father was calling. Her eyes rolled upward. Kemp's third eye was open for sure because each time Anya got in trouble, Khelani was having doubts about hustling or anything of that nature, he would call. Too many times she thought about how life would be if she stopped hustling and just gave a relationship with Kyrie a shot. Then she'd think about him playing her or cheating on her, and all bets would be off.

"Hi daddy."

"Hey Baby Girl. How is everything going?"

"Everything is good." She dared not tell him about Anya's drama. Since he cut her off, he hadn't asked about her, and Khelani hadn't volunteered any information.

"Good. There is a shipment coming in tomorrow. You know the drill. Send Kasim and Delante to retrieve it."

"Got it."

"You sure everything is okay? You need anything?"

"I'm sure dad. We had the issue with Delante being robbed, but that's been handled. I've secured a new customer. Things are running smoothly."

"I appreciate you my dear. To show you how much so, I am depositing a check from my company into your account for $20,000. On record, it shows as a signing bonus for your promotion in my company. Take the money and buy yourself something nice."

"Thank you, dad. I appreciate that."

"Anything for you my dear. I love you."

"I love you too."

Khelani and her father ended their conversation and she leaned against the island in the kitchen. She may as well push her anger to the side and get her work done because as soon as the sun went down, she was going to bust Camila's ass.

KYRIE WALKED into Camila's office with an expression on his face that was void of emotion. She had called him crying earlier, and he really almost ignored her. When Camila was desperate, she'd go through great lengths to get her way. She could cry at the drop of a dime, yet here he was trying to see what she wanted. Kyrie refused to go back on the tough love he was giving her. Camila sat behind her desk with a puffy face.

"What's wrong with you?" he asked.

"Kyrie, I fucked up bad. I haven't paid the light bill for the past two months and in order to avoid disconnection, I had to pay $1625 today. On top of that, the liquor inventory came today, and I had to pay $7,021 for that. I'm dead ass broke Kyrie, and the rent on my condo is due in three days. Please just give me some coke to move, and I swear every dollar will be accounted for."

He didn't even blink. "If you don't know how to run a business, I suggest you hire someone to do it for you, or you let this club go. You already owe me money. It's not my job to bail you out."

Camila's mouth fell open from shock. She couldn't believe that Kyrie was treating her like this. Before she could respond, one of her bouncers came through on the walkie talkie that they used to communicate with.

"Camila, there's a female at the front of the club that's demanding to see you."

Camila hissed as she stood up. "Who in the fuck is demanding to see me?"

Kyrie followed her to the front of the club, because he planned on leaving. Camila wasn't talking about shit. All she wanted to do was beg, and he didn't have shit for her. Kyrie stopped to speak to someone that he knew since patrons had begun to enter the club and by the time he exited the club, he was shocked to hear Khelani yelling in Camila's face.

"Bitch for what you did to my sister, I'm gon' beat yo' ass." She hit Camila in the face and by the time her second punch landed, security was grabbing her.

Khelani wasn't the hair pulling type, but she was furious

that the fight was being broken up before she could do what she wanted to do, so anger made her grab Camila's hair. She wouldn't let it go for shit. The bouncer tried to pry her hands off Camila's tracks, but she wasn't budging. She then attempted to hit Camila with an uppercut. Khelani was out for blood. After a good three minutes, she finally let Camila's hair go, and Camila tried to charge her, but security grabbed her, and Kyrie grabbed Khelani.

"Chill! Fuck is you doing? That's my cousin," Kyrie declared.

Khelani's head jerked back. "I don't give a fuck! That whore and her friend jumped my sister, and she has to see me. You can't fuckin' save her."

Kyrie shook his head. He wasn't trying to get in the middle of female business. Camila could be a messy muhfucka, but he couldn't let her be attacked in his presence. "Khelani ju—"

"Nigga fuck what you talking about," she spat. No one could save Camila. Not even Kyrie.

Before he could speak, he heard a popping sound, and a look of shock registered on Khelani's face. He heard people scream just as Khelani fell forward. It took him a second to realize that she'd been shot. His eyes scanned her body until his gaze fell on a bloody stain on her shirt near the top of her abdomen. Kyrie's eyes darted out into the sea of people scattering and as he held Khelani in his arms, he saw the nigga that robbed his artist of his chain fleeing the scene with a gun in his hand.

To be continued...

Excerpt from The Plug's Girl:

By Natisha Raynor

ONE

Dion let out a light squeal as she stretched her body. When she couldn't stretch it any further, she held the position for a moment, then opened her eyes and let out a deep sigh. She'd had the best night's sleep ever. Being in the third year of her medical residency was no joke. She'd worked sixteen days in a row and just when she thought her body wouldn't be able to take anymore, she realized that it was time for her to take her vacation. Seven days without having to see Duke University Hospital sounded like heaven to her. Dion turned on her left side and grabbed her phone from the nightstand.

"Geesh," her eyebrows shot up when she saw that it was noon. She hadn't slept that late in a long time.

Gazing up at the ceiling she realized that she only had a few hours before she was to be at her parents' house for an early dinner. A noise resembling that of the low growl of an animal coming from her abdomen caused Dion to chuckle. She wouldn't be able to last without food for a few hours, so she kicked the covers back and padded to her kitchen. Dion's mother hadn't cooked a big meal in months, so she wondered what the special occasion was.

Dion figured that maybe they just wanted to be able to question her extensively about her personal life without her being able to rush them off the phone. Dion loved her parents with all of her heart, but sometimes their overprotectiveness was a little much to put up with. Being that she was the only child, not even being twenty-four years old was enough for them to back off. All of her life she'd been a good kid. One that loved to read, was never disrespectful, never got in trouble, and made her parents proud. She even stepped up to the plate and started helping them financially once she started her first year of residency. Her mother's health started to decline, and she was unable to work. Her father also had to stop working much sooner than expected and being that he found jobs getting paid under the table when he first came to the states, his SSI benefits weren't as much as his wife's. The decrease in income put them in a real bind. After paying the mortgage each month and the utilities there was hardly any money left over for medication, food, and household supplies. That's where Dion stepped up to the plate.

Taking on the extra responsibility wasn't exactly easy for Dion, but she'd never see her parents struggling. She was just glad that they didn't start needing her assistance until she had graduated from college and was no longer a struggling college student. At least her residency was a paid one, so she had money coming in. Her parents only needed her help for about a year, and then her father told her something about an increase in his benefits.

Dion had wanted to be a doctor ever since she was a child. She was born in the states, but she saw pictures and she heard stories of her parents' poor upbringing in Haiti. As soon as

Dion's mother was able to find someone to watch her that didn't charge an arm and a leg, she went back to work at a tire factory. A job that sometimes offered overtime, and Clara always took advantage. There were times she'd work sixteen hour shifts and her husband hated to see his wife working such long hours, so he applied for a job there as well. That way he could be the one working the overtime while his wife went home to their child. The long, tedious, hours were hell on his body, but the paychecks made it all worth it. Nothing made Robert more proud than to be able to save up for his daughter's college. With a lot of hard work, student loans, and scholarships from her good grades, Dion was not only going to be a doctor, but she was first person in her family to graduate from college. No sooner than she started her residency, her father's body gave out on him. A heart attack took him out of work for good.

After a quick breakfast of oatmeal and strawberries, Dion brushed her teeth, showered, and put on a gray sweatshirt dress with black thigh high boots. As she stood in the mirror taking out her twists, Dion observed her toasted almond complexion and made a mental note to schedule a facial. Her naturally long lashes made her light brown eyes pop. As Dion ran her tongue over her stark white teeth, she also made a mental note to go shopping. For the past few years, Dion had been a smooth size twelve. Standing at 5'6 she had a nice round ass and big thick thighs. However, in the past few months, she'd shed at least fifteen pounds from constant walking at the hospital and some days being so busy she could barely squeeze in the time to eat. She hadn't tried to lose the weight on purpose but since she did, she needed some new clothes. It would be a small treat to herself. Aside from the trip she was going on to Cancun with her best friend, all Dion ever really did was work.

When she first began losing weight, she told herself there wasn't a need for clothes, because she barely went anywhere, but Dion was tired of wasting her life away. There had to be more to life than work and sleep. She knew what being a doctor would entail, but she never expected to be spending some of the best years of her life doing nothing but working then coming home to read a book or watch a movie. Using her fingers, Dion fluffed out the jet black coils that touched her shoulders. Her hair was super thick and when straightened, it touched the middle of her back. After adding gold hoops to her ears and a watch to her wrist, Dion grabbed her purse and keys and headed out to her champagne colored Camry. She liked her car, and it was only four years old, but Dion thought about maybe gifting herself a really nice luxury car for her twenty-fifth birthday in six months. She didn't study her ass off to become a doctor to live mediocre. Not that there was anything wrong with a Camry, but there was also nothing wrong with spoiling yourself.

Dion's one bedroom apartment was only fifteen minutes away from her job, but it was almost thirty minutes away from her parents' house. She blasted rapper Lil' Baby all the way there. When Dion pulled up in her parents' driveway, her eyebrows furrowed in confusion. Her parents rarely had company and when they did, it was friends from church or neighbors.

"Who in the hell do my parents know with a Maybach?" Dion had never seen one in person, and she for damn sure didn't think the first time she ever saw one would be at her parents' house. What was even stranger, was that there was also a black Escalade parked on the street in front of the house.

Where did all these nice ass cars come from? Better yet, who was inside? When her parents invited her over for dinner, they never mentioned other people being there. Both her parents had a few family members in the states, but there weren't a lot of them. Dion got used to growing up with minimal family around. The last time she could even recall her parents having company was after her father had a heart attack and a few members of the church came by to bring food and give their well wishes.

Dion wasted no time getting out of the car because she was just that curious to know who was inside. As she closed her car door, she eyed the Maybach and had to admit that it looked like pure money. It was an exquisite vehicle indeed and even with her in the process of becoming a doctor, she knew she'd never buy herself a car that expensive. Dion didn't have to knock because she had a key. The small two bedroom house that she grew up in was modest, but it was home. It was filled with memories and always smelled good whether it was from the sweets her mother stayed baking or the different incense that she burned. When Dion pushed open the front door and stepped over the threshold, the first thing she noticed was the smell.

The cologne and the perfume combined invaded her nostrils. The scents were dominating the air that she breathed and were both masculine, feminine, and expensive smelling. Dion's eyes swept over the three people that occupied her parents' couch. The first person she saw was handsome as all the fuck. She couldn't tell his height since he was seated, but she could tell he was tall. His skin was the color of cinnamon, and his thick long locs were doing their own thing. His sharp nose and high cheekbones gave him a regal look, but the tattoo on his neck and the ones that decorated his arms gave him a thuggish appeal. The watch that adorned his wrist looked to be just as exquisite and expensive as the Maybach parked out front, and Dion would bet money that he was the one driving it. The man was dressed in designer from head to toe, and when their eyes locked, he only held her gaze for a moment. His eyes then slid down the length of her body as he sized her up.

"Dion hi dear," her mother got up from the recliner that she was seated in and went over to her daughter with a nervous chuckle just as Dion's eyes landed on a beautiful woman.

She had the same cinnamon colored skin as the man seated on the left of her, and she had a colorful headwrap on her head that hid her tresses. Red lipstick painted her full lips, and she was dressed in a black dress that hugged her frame. Black stockings covered her legs, and on her feet were red pointy toe heels. She looked old enough to be the man's mother, but she was very pretty and the way she sat up straight with her head held high let Dion know that wherever she went, her presence commanded attention. The expression on her face was serious and her cat like eyes zeroed in on Dion and looked her over just as the young man had.

"Hi," Dion turned to her mother. "You didn't tell me we were having guests for dinner."

There was an odd tension in the air that Dion picked up on right away. She didn't like how everyone was staring at her. Her gaze finally landed on her father, and he didn't look well. He could barely look Dion in the eyes, and he was stroking his beard. Something he always did when he was stressed out. Dion suddenly became alarmed. Tearing her eyes away from her father, she peeped the man sitting to the right of the woman she didn't know. His dark skin and piercing eyes, high cheekbones, and serious stare sent chills up her spine. Who in the hell were these people?

"It was kind of a surprise," her mother spoke up with another nervous chuckle. "These are old friends of ours from Haiti. This is Oluah, his wife Vivian, and their son Yasiin."

Dion gave a quick head nod. "Hello. Nice to meet you," she offered a nervous smile still not sure why everyone was acting so weird. If dinner was going to be like this, she'd rather find an excuse to leave. If these people were truly old friends of her parents, why did everyone seem so serious and uncomfortable?

Oluah stood up and walked over to Dion. The way he peered at her made goosebumps appear on her arms. He was giving off quite a few different vibes, but none of them were friendly. His eyes were cold and unwelcoming. Dion didn't miss the way her mother instinctively and protectively moved closer to her, and she wanted to know what in the hell was going on. Oluah's gaze was so intimidating that Dion almost took a step back until a creepy grin eased across his face.

He extended his hand for a shake and Dion hesitantly raised her hand. "I'm not one for beating around the bush, so let me give you proper introductions. I am your future father-in-law, and this," he turned to the side and gestured towards Yasiin. "Is your husband to be."

SNEAK PEAK OF TRAP STAR
ONE

LUCKY ME

A shiny 2012 White Range Rover Sport came to a smooth stop perfectly in the parking space. The vehicle was one of the trappings of success; a symbol of luxury. Behind the wheel sat a young gorgeous African American female named Brianna Campbell. Through her Dolce & Gabbana shades, she glanced down at the platinum Rolex watch on her wrist. It read one o'clock. She was right on time for her hair appointment.

As soon as she entered the hair salon, Brianna noticed that all eyes were on her. Still, she remained cool behind her dark tinted shades. It would take more than a few envious eyes to unnerve her. Although Hera by Him was an upscale hair salon, it wasn't free from the catty gossip that plagued every hood shop. As soon as Brianna strolled past, almost immediately the whispers and speculation began.

With of all the high priced designer accessories and clothes Brianna wore, the majority of the women assumed that she was some ball players' girlfriend or wife. The large six carat diamond ring did little to dispel those rumors. There was no denying that she was well kept. Her outfit and designer bag caused some insecure women to fall back into obscurity when they saw her. They knew all her accessories were real, while most of theirs were bootleg; cheap knock offs.

Usually all clients were required to wait in the sitting area until they were called by their stylist, but not Brianna. She strolled right pass the receptionist, heading straight to the back. The receptionist merely glanced at Brianna, but she didn't attempt to stop her. She recognized that Brianna was a regular. But besides that Brianna had a swagger about her that suggested that she wasn't to be messed with.

Her stylist seemed to light up when she saw Brianna coming towards her. It wasn't because she was happy to see her or that liked doing her hair either. Brianna paid well; it was as simple as that. The stylist knew that she wouldn't have to do another head that day. Once Brianna was done tipping her, she was going to be straight.

"Hey Bri." The stylist happily said. "I can set my watch to you girl, you always on time. I wish all my clients were like you."

Lauren was one of the few people Brianna knew she could never allow to get a peek into her life. She had witnessed first hand the way Lauren spoke about her other clients and their personal business. So no matter how friendly her stylist was to her, Brianna was always the same; nonchalant. She always gave her the cold shoulder, shutting down any attempts at them becoming too friendly. All the idle chit-chat that went on between stylist and client didn't exist when she took her seat in the stylist's chair. Brianna guarded her privacy like a celebrity. Brianna simply smiled in response to the comment.

After taking off her shades and placing them inside her bag, she handed her personal items to her stylist, who put the bag under the counter.

In the mirror Lauren smiled as she examined different parts of Brianna's weave. She could feel Brianna watching her. She went from the front to the back inspecting her hair. When she reached the back she grimaced slightly. Thankfully Brianna didn't catch it.

A large scar on the back of Brianna's head had caused this reaction. Brianna's scar betrayed her pampered appearance. What in the world was a woman of Brianna's stature doing with such an ungodly scar was beyond Lauren. As a matter of fact it was the subject of debate whenever Brianna left the salon. To her credit the stylist never asked any questions, and Brianna never offered an explanation.

Lauren could tell she had been through some shit, but what she didn't know. She would have loved to find out.

Quickly pushing those thoughts out of her mind, she went to work. Meanwhile, Brianna casually looked around. While Lauren moved about in the booth Brianna took notice of her attire. She was dressed in a black t-shirt and black jeans. Brianna looked down to see what she had on her feet and instantly she got pissed.

"Fuckin' Jordan's!' She cursed to herself.

Those sneakers would be forever stoned in Brianna's memory. It didn't matter if they were worn by a male or female, she hated them. As she closed her eyes Brianna's mind began to trace back to the moment that she had not been able to erase. Suddenly her thoughts began to run wild.

The halogen headlights shone brightly from the four door European sedan, illuminating the entire garage. With a touch of a button, the garage door quickly closed. Calmly the two occupants of the car made their exit. Tre led the way inside the house. After placing his key into the lock, he entered the house and punched in his security code, deactivating the alarm. His girlfriend Brianna followed closely behind. The couple had just come home from a busy night on the town. Brianna loved going out, she like being in the spot light. But Tre was the total opposite. In Tre's line of work it was better to be talked about rather than seen.

The streets of Charlotte, NC were like a jungle, filled with both predators and prey. But by no means was Tre anybody's prey. On the contrary, he was just as dangerous as they came. But, to meet Tre for the first time one would never know. He had a very laid back disposition, and would rarely be seen in jeans or any of the latest urban wear. He had learned along time ago, that the quieter you were the easier it was to move.

Inside the luxurious confines of his townhouse, Tre breathed a sigh of relief. .

"Umm, that steak was good as shit!" he suddenly announced. "I'm full like a motherfucker."

He flopped down on the couch, kicked back and relaxed. Reaching for the television remote, he turned on the 63 inch plasma TV. Quickly he became captivated by the new Rick Ross video that was airing on BET. He was feeling extremely sluggish. The big meal he had eaten had begun to take effect.

Meanwhile, in the hallway Brianna began to get comfortable herself. She slipped off her high heel shoes, loosened the buttons on her blouse and made her way toward the living room.

"Hold on Big Poppa." Brianna said. "Don't go to sleep on me yet. I got something way better than that steak!"

To Tre that could only mean one thing, some good head. Like the old saying went, 'The way to a man's heart may have been through a man's stomach'. But for Tre it was threw his dick. He went fool over some good head. And nobody did it better, than Brianna.

Immediately, Brianna got down on her knees and went to work. Quickly she unzipped Tre's pants, reaching inside she gripped his dick, pulled it out and took it into her mouth. Brianna's mouth was warm and wet. She began licking and sucking on the head of his dick. She worked her way down until every inch was in her mouth. Moving faster and faster until she felt his dick grow harder and harder. Brianna used just the right amount of spit and suction. Tre drop his head back and sighed.

Again and again, he thrust his hips to meet her hungry mouth. With his eyes closed he enjoyed the moment.

"Damn baby Suck dat dick!" He cursed. "Do dat shit."

Tre's cursing didn't even bother Brianna. She was with whatever it took to get him off. She knew if she didn't, there were plenty other hoes, out in the streets, who would jump at the opportunity. She felt if he was going to stray, it wasn't going to be because of anything she did or didn't do.

"Cum in my mouth daddy!" Brianna demanded.

The commandment drove Tre crazy. He quickly obliged. A hot jolt of semen shot from his balls to the head of his dick, into Brianna's warm and waiting mouth. As soon as it came out, she gobbled it up and swallowed it down. When she had drained every last drop of his love juice, Brianna continued to suck on his dick. Unable to take any more, Tre tried to pry her lips off.

"Alright, God damn!" He exclaimed. "Brianna, that's enough."

From the floor, Brianna glanced up at her man. A sinister smile spread across her face. She knew it was a job well done.

Getting up off her knees, Brianna proudly stood above her man.

"Nigga, git up." She joked. "It wasn't all like that."

Tre lay on the couch in the fetal position, trying to regain the little bit of energy, he had just lost.

"Shiiitttttt!!!" Was all he managed to say.

Brianna insisted. "C'mon, Tre stop playin'. Git up and come wit me upstairs to the shower. Let's get ready for bed. "

"You go 'head." He told her. "I'll be up there in a minute."

"Promise."

"Promise!" He replied. "I'll be right up there as soon as I get myself together."

"Alright, hurry up!" She demanded. "We ain't finished yet. We got one more round to go."

Reluctantly, Brianna walked away to prepare for their next sexual romp to take place in the shower. She hurried along in anticipation of what was to come. She had just turned the corner, taking only a few steps out of the living room when suddenly two masked gunmen appeared.

With the barrel of a semi-automatic weapon pointed directly at her forehead, Brianna didn't utter a word. Instinctively, she backed up as the gunmen moved silently toward her. The TV successfully drowned out any noise they made.

Quickly, the two masked men pushed Brianna into the living room, brandishing their weapons on Tre. Caught completely off guard, Tre just stared in disbelief, wondering how in the hell had these two niggas gotten into his house without setting off the alarm system.

The larger one barked. "Nigga, make a move and I'm gonna let you feel this heat."

Immediately, the other man snatched up Brianna. Everything appeared to be moving in slow motion to her.

Brianna was violently shoved onto the couch. With a gun pointed in her face, she couldn't do anything but stare. The gunman and his weapon were oblivious to her, for whatever reason her eyes were locked on the man's hand. All she could see was the word 'Smalls' in cursive writing tattooed on the bottom of his hand.

"Bitch, don't look at me!" The gunman growled. "Turn ya fuckin head'!"

Either Brianna moved too slowly or it wasn't fast enough. Whatever the case was the gunman, viciously slapped her. Brianna head recoiled violently from the blow. She fell back onto the couch with the taste of blood quickly filling her mouth.

"Ok, you know what it is. Just give us what we came for." The larger one demanded. "Now where the stash at?"

"Nigger ain't nuttin' here!" Tre snapped. "I don't eat where I shit."

Unfortunately, the gunmen didn't buy a word he was saying. Without warning the large man, began to pistol whipped Tre. He was thrown to the floor where he was kicked and beaten some more. Blood began to flow freely from a gash in his head.

"Nigga, you think this a muthafuckin' game huh?" He yelled. "Now, I'ma ask you one more time. Where is it at?"

By now Brianna was in a state of shock. She didn't understand why Tre didn't just give them what they wanted so they could leave. She thought it was just that simple.

"Look, I already told you niggas. Ain't nuttin' here." He muttered through a pair of swollen lips.

A third man entered the room. With a nod of his head, he motion to the one who had Brianna, to lift her up. His partner reacted by reaching down, grabbing a handful of Brianna's hair, and snatching her up off the couch. He placed one arm around her neck, the other hand clutched the gun that was pressed to her temple.

"Nigga, you better tell us what we wanna hear and fast." The other gunman spat. "The next muthafuckin' lie you tell, this bitch is dead! Now, where's the stash at?"

Though he was more than a little woozy, Tre was still defiant. He glared angrily at his two assailants. An evil thought ran through his mind, 'If I can get to one of my guns. I'm going to kill these motherfuckers.

Amongst all the commotion, the shouting, the threats and the violence, the videos were still playing on the television, a tomb like silence suddenly enveloped the room. The threat of death hung in the air.

For what seemed like an eternity no one said a word. Brianna eyes suddenly locked with Tre's. They seemed to sing a sad song. They pleaded with Tre to give up the goods. Still he stood his ground, refusing to say a thing.

Seeing this Brianna knew she would be forced to take matters into her own hands. She felt it was the only way to remedy the situation, since Tre wasn't talking.

"It's upstairs in the bedroom." She blurted out. "The money is upstairs in the bedroom in a suitcase."

'Damn!' Tre cursed to himself. He shot her an ice cold stare.

Tre would have rather her give up the location of the dope than the money. Money was too hard to come by. Now he had to take some more pen chances to recoup his cash. While if he was robbed of some drugs, he could go to his drug connection and get more on consignment.

The gunmen released his grip on Brianna, who stood there holding her throat. Trying to recover from the choke hold she had been in. Taking two steps away from her, suddenly the gunmen turned back around and viciously struck her with the butt of his gun. Caught off guard, Brianna went crashing face first to the floor. She was knocked unconscious by a blow to her temple.

The other two gunmen laughed heartily, signaling their approval.

"Damn, you knocked that bitch out cold." one commented. "Now go upstairs and get the money."

Doing as he was told, the second gunman fled the living room, and went to retrieve the money.

The larger gunman announced, "Nigga, ya girl smarter than you. You lucky she told us when she did. I thought we was gonna have to kill her ass, just for you to talk. Just for that we gonna let ya'll live."

Tre didn't believe a word the man had said. But he wasn't really focused on him anyway. It was the third man who didn't speak a word that concerned him the most. It was obvious he was the one running things.

Before Tre could give it any real thought or get himself together to mount an attack, he heard the other gunman come running down the stairs. It was then that he realized that he may have blown his only chance of survival.

"You got it?"

"Yeah, I got it! It was right where she said it was." He laughed.

Tre watched as the other gunman entered the room and gave the bag to third man. At that point he sensed that something was up, though no more words were exchanged between the men. It was as if he knew what was about to happen.

With two large caliber firearms trained on him, Tre watched as the men inched closer and closer, until they were within pointblank range. Something came over him that he hadn't felt in years, it was fear. Though he had personally sent countless individuals to the afterlife, now that it was his turn, suddenly he realized he didn't want to go. He wasn't ready to leave this earth, not at the ripe old age of twenty five years old. He had so much more living to do and things to see. He couldn't believe it was ending like this.

Tre wasn't a chump, but he knew he didn't want to die.

With the finality of the situation close at hand, Tre finally backed down off his defiant stance, his lumped shoulders now suggested he had gone into submission. A pitiful look appeared on his face, one that invited any act of divine intervention. Tre's look invited any act of mercy, so that his life and that of his girlfriend might be spared.

The gunmen shot him a cold look of indifference, one that seemed to suggest that they would not deviate from their plan. Their hard core looks condemn him and his girlfriend to their fate, which was death.

Suddenly without warning, Tre lunged for one of gunman's firearms. If he was going to die, he wasn't going down without a fight. Too bad he wasn't quite fast enough to execute his plans. Gunshots exploded through the room. Six bullets found their mark. When the smoke cleared Tre was slumped on the floor, dead.

"Now, finish the bitch! And let's get the fuck outta here!" The first gunman screamed.

Standing above Brianna, he had a chance to see her innocent beauty. Even though she was covered in blood, her face was captivating. He closed his eyes and fired two shots, one missed badly and other drew blood, but it only grazed her head.

Brianna lay motionless on the floor. The gunman thought he had successfully executed her.

Long after the gunmen were gone, Brianna continued to lie on the floor, playing dead. She wanted to be sure no one was going to double back, to finish the job. As she looked around, she saw Tre's lifeless body lying in a pool of blood. For a long time she lay there thinking about Tre. It was heartbreaking to see him like that. Though he was certainly no angel Tre didn't deserve to go out like that.

That night at the hospital, a weeping Brianna sat for hours answering every question that the police threw at her.

"Ma'am, could you tell us why someone would want to hurt you and your fiancé?" The older white cop asked.

"You said robbery earlier, but it didn't seem like they took anything of value." The other cop spoke.

Brianna knew she couldn't tell them exactly what happen, there were still drugs at the house. And she didn't know how much. She cleverly sprinkled lies in with the truth. She knew she needed to get home and get the dope out the house. Or she would not only be losing Tre, but possibly her freedom. The FEDS didn't care who did the time as long as someone did it.

When the police left, Brianna checked herself out the hospital. She couldn't bring herself to stay in the house that night. So she checked herself into a hotel. While she lay on the bed, she looked up at the ceiling. She wished she had a family to lean on, but she knew hers was not an option. Her family life had never been what a little girl deserved. Especially one who had both parents. This was now her second time, being alone, and having no one to turn too. As she fell asleep she reflected on her childhood.

TWO

Hard knock life

Brianna Campbell always has been a dreamer. She loved fairytales with happy endings. Ever since she was a child she loved to pretend. Brianna was a latchkey child, raised on unhealthy amount of television and movies. She idolized black actors and actresses, to the point that she could quote and re-enact some of the most famous parts, line for line. Her room was like a sanctuary.

Life in the Campbell household wasn't the same for Brianna as it was for her two other younger siblings, Jonathan and Charrise. Almost from day one, she sensed that there was preferential treatment shown to her younger sister and brother. It wasn't until she was around nine years old that she found out the reason why. At Brianna's ninth birthday party things finally came to a head. And the truth was revealed.

———

"How old are you now? How old are you now..." The partygoers chanted.

In the darkened kitchen, the nine candles on the store bought chocolate birthday cake, illuminated the room. Brianna hovered dangerously close to the cake, staring into the candles as if she were hypnotized. She enjoyed being the birthday girl, the center of attention. Sadly, she knew that her moment in the spotlight would fade quickly. Still she lived in the moment. Like any good actress, Brianna played her part well. Outwardly, she grinned ear to ear at her adoring guests. Inwardly, she hurt badly.

As she scanned the room, looking at each familiar face, one was noticeably absent, her Dad's. For some strange reason, he never participated in anything dealing with her. By now, it was routine, still it didn't hurt any less. She always noticed that he constantly shied away from her. Often Brianna wondered what she had done to deserve this.

"Brianna blow out the candles baby and make a wish!" Her mother urged her.

"Ok."

Inhaling deeply, Brianna summoned all the air her tiny

lungs could hold and blew out the candles. Momentarily the kitchen went pitch black; the partygoers began to cheer loudly. When the lights came back on tears could be seen running down Brianna's rosy cheeks. Despite how it appeared, these weren't tears of joy.

"Oh, look at her she's so happy she's crying." One parent suggested.

But Lorraine Campbell knew otherwise. If there was one thing she knew, it was her children. She knew their temperaments and tendencies. And this was completely out of character for Brianna. She wasn't emotional at all. Lorraine sensed that something was very wrong.

Gently her mother took Brianna by the hand, and whisked her away from her guests. She led her straight to the bathroom.

"What's wrong with you?" She asked. "What are you crying for?"

Though she tried her best to keep her composure, Brianna couldn't. Her tears continued to flow freely, now her body was racked by long hard sobs. Young Brianna merely stood in front of her mother unsure of what to say or do.

Her mother replied, "Don't just stand there looking all sorry. Say something! How else will I know what's the matter with you?"

After shedding a few more tears, finally Brianna mustered up the courage to tell her mother exactly what was bothering her.

"Where my Daddy?" She began. "How come he never comes to my birthday parties, huh? He always here for Jonathan's and Charrise's."

Her question caught Lorraine off guard. She hadn't expected this at all. But in the back of her mind she knew this day would come.

It was Lorraine's turn to be dumbfounded. She didn't know

where to begin. But she knew that she had some explaining to do and fast.

"Brianna," She began. "The man you know as your father is not your father. He's your sister's father and your brother's father. But he's not your father."

Brianna exclaimed, "Huh? I don't believe you. You're a liar mommy!"

Brianna began to have a temper tantrum, she flailed her arms wildly at her mother. Dozens of light blows rained down on her mother's mid-section.

Unable to control her daughter's violent outburst, Lorraine reached down and viciously slapped Brianna across her face. This seemed to bring her back to reality. Pain exploded across her cheek. She stopped her antics and clutched the side of her face.

Through clenched teeth her mother spoke, "Listen Miss and listen good. Herman is not your father. He is nothing to you. You and him have no blood relations. And that's that!"

Though Brianna couldn't comprehend everything her mother had said. But she understood enough. She got the message loud and clear. From that moment on Brianna was forced to grow up fast. She didn't like her mother's explanation but she had to accept it. For now it would be the only one she would get. It would be years before she knew the whole story.

Her mother and her stepfather, Herman, were high school sweethearts. When Herman went off to the army, following graduation, Lorraine had gotten weak and had a one night stand. Brianna was the product of that affair. But since Herman came home on leave around the same time she had gotten pregnant, and they too had intercourse, she chose to blame Herman for the paternity of the child.

The other guy was a local thug, who had nothing going for himself, other than being handsome. On the other hand,

154

Herman had plans and goals that he was working towards. He was merely using the military as a stepping stone.

Some years later, unable to deal with her guilty conscious any more, Lorraine admitted her mistake to her husband. She received a severe beating as a reward for her honesty. Still Herman couldn't bring himself to leave his family. Against his better judgment, he stayed. Herman too was the product of a broken home. To his credit, he wouldn't let one act of infidelity break up his happy home.

Even though Herman had forgiven Lorraine, he could never forget. Everyday he was reminded of her infidelity when he looked at Brianna. He grew to despise her. As the years went on, he became abusive towards her. Not physically but mentally. Sometimes that was just as bad. His harsh words stung Brianna.

'You ain't cute. I don't know what you stay in the mirror for all day?' he commented. 'You ain't shit! And you ain't never gonna be shit! Your sorry ass daddy wasn't shit! Look he don't even care about you!'

Brianna was an A/B student, passing her classes with flying colors. One marking period she hadn't done so well. She received two C's. And her stepfather seized the opportunity to criticize and degrade her.

He spat, "Look at this shit here! You're so stupid. How you gonna fail gym?"

Her stepfather had degraded her time and time again, right in front of her mother. When she looked to her mother for support, she got none. Not once did her mother come to her aid and defend her. She did what she always did; Lorraine pretended not to hear it. Little by little, this caused Brianna to have animosity and resentment towards her mother.

Since Herman had money, he got away with murder around the house. Lorraine tolerated his cruelty towards her daughter because he was a good provider. A local businessman, Herman owned a string of soul food restaurants throughout Charlotte. She was just as much a dependent as her children were on her husband. She dared not voice her opinion in any way shape or form. She did her best to avoid the wrath of Herman. Lorraine knew when Herman got mad he got even financially by withholding funds.

Even though her younger sister and brother weren't nearly as bright as her, they always seemed to get the benefit of the doubt. When they failed a class, they failed because the teacher didn't like them. When she failed it was because she was just too dumb.

Over the course of time, her stepfather succeeded in slowly stripping her of her self-esteem. Brianna's grades began to suffer. She became a prisoner in her own home. She chose only to leave her room for one of three things, to go to school, use the bathroom and to eat. She avoided her stepfather as if he had an infectious disease.

Lorraine felt her daughter's pain, but truthfully she was powerless to stop the abuse. With her husband's blessing she decided to seek out Brianna's father. Secretly Herman had hoped that the girl's father would take her to live with him.

One day, Lorraine walked into her daughter's room and surprised Brianna. She told her to hurry up and get dressed, that her father was coming over to meet her. Instantly Brianna's face lit up, she felt reinvigorated as if a burden had been lifted off her.

Brianna got dressed in her best clothes, she raced downstairs and sat on the front porch eagerly awaiting her dad. Each passing car carried Brianna's hopes for a better life. And with each passing car, she was devastated more and more. Hours went by, with no sign of her father. Still Brianna didn't move from that spot, she never gave of hope. She sat there until the sun began to set. Finally, her mother had seen enough, she summoned Brianna inside the house. Lorraine was just as disappointed and heartbroken as she.

"C'mon in the house, Bri. That nigga ain't coming!" She cursed. "Don't worry about it baby. He missed out on a good thing not meeting you. It's gonna be alright! I promise, it's gonna be alright!"

Her mother's reassuring words did nothing for her. If anything they contributed to her ill feelings. Silently she cursed the day she was born. All she ever wanted was a mother and a father. Was that too much to ask for?

Tears began to well up in Brianna eyes. Suddenly she took off like a rocket, racing up the stairs. When she reached the second floor, she spotted her stepfather exiting the bathroom. He had a shit eating grin pasted to his face as their eyes met.

Brianna continued to run, racing past him to her room. She slammed the door and locked it. Throwing herself on the bed, she cried herself to sleep.

All throughout her formative years, Brianna had to endure this treatment. She became a stranger in her own house to everyone but her younger sister Charrise. The two had to keep their friendship a secret. She was the only person in her household that showed her genuine kindness. Maybe she wasn't going to be shit after all.

The Westside of Charlotte had long been a breeding ground for top flight hustlers and ruthless killers. That was where Treshaun Ellis, aka Tre, hailed from; LaSalle Street, the Betty's Ford section to be specific.

Almost from the time he was born, his life revolved around the streets. Both of Tre's parents were hustlers. His father

Wally was a low level drug dealer. And his mother Marva was a booster, who stole clothes, for the entire neighborhood to buy. At one point or another, one or both of Tre's parents were in prison serving time for their parts in some botched crime. Subsequently, young Tre was raised by his maternal grand-mother, on and off.

A day young Tre would never forget was the day his parents were killed. Fresh out of prison, Marva was looking extremely beautiful; Wally concocted a scheme to make money. He sent her out into the nightclubs of Charlotte, with form fitting clothes, in search of hustlers. Marva would then bed the hustlers, sexing them on a regular basis. As she did so, she gathered information on them. Like where they lived, what kind of guns they had or how much money was in the house. Their plan met success the first few times. Wally and his friend successfully robbed a few weak hustlers. With each conquest, the couple grew greedy for more.

Word had quickly spread on the street about the duo. They had gone to the well one too many times. After robbing one big time hustler, a hit was placed on them. Shortly after the order was given, Wally and Marva were found dead in the trunk of a car. They were both shot execution style in the back of the head. There were no witnesses to the crime and police never captured the triggerman.

Death seemed to further complicate Tre's already nomadic life, leaving a void in it. The murder of his parent's left him feeling more vulnerable and more broken than ever. He grew up thinking life wasn't fair.

From that point on, young Tre knew that life had no happy endings in store for him. He figured that his life could be only what he made of it. With both sources of income gone, Tre slowly began to gravitate towards the street. His neighborhood was filled with negativity and eventually he felt obliged to engage in it.

Originally, Tre got into the game to provide for, not only himself, but his grandmother too. He saw her struggling for the basic necessities, food, clothing and shelter. He didn't want to become another added burden upon her.

Around that time, Tre began to have a strange fascination with streets. With negativity all around him, he began to look up to the local drug dealers. They had money, the finer things in life, jewelry, pretty women and expensive rides that they flaunted on a regular basis. There was one drug dealer in particular that Tre idolized, named Petey. Tre worshipped the ground Petey walked on. After all, Petey was a ghetto superstar.

Petey believed that life came down to dollars and cents; either you had money or you didn't. It was as simple as that. He was prepared to hustle to get it.

Only five years older than Tre, Petey carried himself like a much older hustler. Just like Tre, he came from a family of hustlers; his daddy ran a pool-hall speakeasy and his older brother was a dope boy. Petey's entire family was involved in the game, in one way or another. It was almost expected that he would follow suit. And when he did no one even raised an eyebrow.

Out of all the kids in the neighborhood, Petey took a liking to Tre. This was because Tre would do anything he asked of him. Petey was no fool, he knew a soldier when he saw one. For the disenfranchised black youths like Tre, he was a godsend.

Petey was a smooth dude, he was a lover and fighter, a gangster and a gentleman all rolled up into one. He was everything Tre wanted to be. But most of all he was a character who had game for days. There was always a reason behind everything he did.

"Nigga, you got some money in ya pockets?" He would always ask.

"No." Tre replied. "I ain't got nothin'."

"Here's a lil sumthin' sumthin'!"

From a thick wad of bills, Petey peeled off a crisp twenty dollar bill and hand it to Tre. His eyes lit up, like it was Christmas. There had never been a time in his life that anyone just given him something without expecting something in return. That random act kindness went a long way with Tre. It instilled a sense of loyalty in him for Petey. From that day forward, no one could ever say anything bad about Petey; not around him. Talking bad about Petey was like talking bad about his late mother.

Petey became like a big brother or mentor of sorts. Soon Tre became his sidekick, his 'little partner' as Petey referred to him as. Before Tre knew it he was running errands for him. Half of the time he didn't know the danger he was in. Tre became a drug courier, helping to distribute Petey's poison all over town.

For his efforts Tre received little or no money. Petey gave him just enough so that Tre would always need him. When it came to the drug game Petey passed along whatever wisdom he could impart and Tre soaked it all up like a sponge.

Like so many other young black males in the neighborhood, Tre viewed the drug game as his ticket out of the ghetto. He immersed himself in the murky, shark infested waters. Sink or swim, he was all in.

"Look nigga, you gotta always make sure you got a least three broads on ya team. The first broad she ain't a hood chick, should either work or go to school getting' an education. She wants somethin' out of life. That's your future wife. The second broad is a soldier; she holds the money and the work at her crib. She gotta be trustworthy. That's your vice president; if somethin should happen to you then she can take over. And the third broad she just a hood rat, somebody from the neighborhood you can keep the product at her house if needed. Even turn her house into a dope house if necessary." Petey explained.

These were rules to the game that Tre would always remember. He knew that they were tried and true because he watched Petey implement them everyday. As time went on Tre became more valuable to Petey. He carefully played his position while patiently waiting his turn.

Sadly just like everyone else Tre ever loved, Petey died tragically, but not by an assassin's bullet. The word on the street was that Petey was poisoned. Although there was no medical evidence to substantiate such a claim, Tre had his suspicions. Women were Petey's Achilles heel; he was never good with them. So Tre trying to find the killer to avenge him was like finding a needle in a haystack. Petey had too many.

Tre had been the one to find Petey and rush him to the hospital. He was there at the hospital, along with a few members of Petey's family, when in the predawn stillness, he took his last labored breath.

The mournful sounds of his mother's cries, along with the steady bleeps and hisses of the life support machines, could be heard throughout the room. It shattered the eerie silence of death. Unable to bear it, Tre exited the room to mourn his mentor's passing.

Petey's death would prove to be bittersweet to Tre. He was thrust into the role of the man, in the hood. His only wish was that Petey was still alive to see it.

As a result of Petey's passing a bloody drug war ensued. The death toll seemed to mount daily. Dealers were scrambling to takeover the turf that once belonged to him. Quickly Tre had organized a team that took on all comers. When the smoke cleared Tre had emerged victorious. But he would forever be a marked man.

Just like Petey had controlled the neighborhood drug traffic for years, so did Tre. He ruled the neighborhood drug game with an iron fist. His reign of terror enabled him to hold it down for several years by instilling the fear of God in his rivals. Murder was his favorite weapon of intimidation. Whenever there was a problem, he made examples.

Seeking to getaway from the house, on the way home from school Brianna made a short diversion to Eastland Mall. It was a trip that would forever change her life.

For hours, Brianna window shopped at every store from Foot Locker, the Downtown locker room to Marshall's. She dreamed of owning all the name brands that she saw in those stores. Her stepfather treated her like a step-child in every sense of the word. When it came time to buy her school clothes, he made sure she got little or no money. Most times, Brianna's mother would have to take money from the other children's shopping allowance.

Standing outside of one store, Brianna starred at the mannequin that was modeling a cute pink Rocawear tennis skirt with a matching shirt. Unbeknownst to her, a pair of guys had slid up behind and began admiring her body. Even though she was shabbily dressed there was no denying her body or her beauty.

The moment Tre laid eyes on her, it was clear that he was attracted to her. He was smart enough to look pass her less than up to par apparel. He saw what her step father would never see; potential. He was awestruck by her beauty. Tre knew he had to have her.

"You'd look good in that." He said with a playful smirk. "Girl I can see you now."

Brianna simply smiled; she didn't know what else to do. Even at seventeen, she wasn't used to boys approaching her.

"You want that?" He asked. "Say the word and it's yours."

Brianna shot the handsome stranger a perplexed look that seemed to say, 'You can't be serious.' Still she felt she had nothing to lose and everything to gain.

"Well, if you wanna buy it for me, I'll take it." She said meekly.

He replied, "C'mon beautiful let's go get it."

This chance meeting turned into a makeshift shopping spree. Brianna entered the store with intentions on only getting one outfit. Instead she came out with an entire wardrobe.

After they finish shopping Tre took her out to eat. It was there that they learned more about each other. Instantly Tre knew that this was one of the chicks that he needed in his life. He felt that Brianna was wifey material, just like that his mentor Petey had described. She was green to the streets so he knew that he could easy manipulate and mold her. Her good looks were just icing on the cake.

On that day, fate had finally smiled on Brianna. It had brought someone in her life that could not only care for her but support her emotionally. She didn't have that type of support at home. Tre would become her mother and her father. Someone she could turn to in times of need...

Click link to read more.

About the Author

Blake Karrington is an Essence Magazine® #1 Bestselling novelist. More than an author, he's a storyteller who places his readers in action-filled moments. It's in these creative spaces that readers are allowed to get to know his complex characters as if they're really alive.

Most of Blake's titles are centered in the South, in urban settings, that are often overlooked by the mainstream. But through Blake's eyes, readers quickly learn that places like Charlotte, NC can be as gritty as they come. It's in these streets of this oft overlooked world where Blake portrays murderers and thieves alike as believable characters. Without judgment, he weaves humanizing back stories that serve up compelling reasons for why one might choose a life of crime.

Readers of his work, speak of the roller coaster ride of emotions that ensues from feeling anger at empathetic characters who always seem to do the wrong thing at the right time, to keep the story moving forward.

In terms of setting, Blake's stories introduce his readers to spaces they may or may not be used to - streetscapes with unkept, cracked sidewalks where poverty prevails, times are depressed and people are broke and desperate. In Blake storytelling space, morality is so curved that rooting for bad guys to get away with murder can sometimes seem like the right thing for the reader to do - even when it's not.

Readers who connect with Blake find him to be relatable.

Likening him to a bad-boy gone good, they see a storyteller who
writes as if he's lived in the world's he generously shares,
readily conveying his message that humanity is everywhere,
especially in the unlikely, mean streets of cities like Charlotte.

Also by Blake Karrington

BLAKE KARRINGTON COLLECTION

A Thug worth fighting for
Who can I run to
Faith & Trust 1 & 2
Baby please come home to me
Drunk on a thugs love 1&2
God forgives 1&2
Tears in the trap
The King of the south 1&2
Trapstar 1-3
Country girls 1-3
Single ladies 1-4
Confessions of an Urban author
Fallin for a hustler like me 1&2
Counterfeit love 1&2
Beard Gang chronicles 1-3
What kind of Man would I be
Thickums
All or nothing
Love, lies, and consequences
Scheming for love

Blake Karrington Collection

Made in United States
Orlando, FL
21 October 2024

52979697R00093